Printed in Singapore.

Library of Congress Cataloging-in-Publication Data
Hong Kong / edited by John and Kirsten Miller.
p. cm. (Chronicles abroad)
ISBN 0-8118-0680-4
1. Hong Kong—Literary collections. 2. Literature,
Modern—19th century. I. Miller, John, 1959- .
II. Miller, Kirsten. 1963- . III. Series.
PN6071.H725H66 1994
808.8'0325125—dc20

93–48091
CIP

Editing and design: Big Fish Books
Composition: Jennifer Petersen, Big Fish Books

Distributed in Canada by Raincoast Books,
112 East Third Avenue, Vancouver, B.C. V5T 1C8

10 9 8 7 6 5 4 3 2 1

Chronicle Books
275 Fifth Street
San Francisco, CA 94103

Special thanks to Maggie dePagter

and Jeff Greenwald

Contents

André Malraux

EPIGRAPH

HONG-KONG HARBOUR
Nine o'clock

WE HAVE JUST passed the lighthouse. No one thinks of going to sleep. We are all on deck, men and women. Lemonade, whisky and soda. On the waterline, rows of

---

French novelist, critic, and statesman André Malraux had a knack for sniffing out trouble wherever he went: he assisted the revolutionaries during the Chinese upheavals in 1925, flew planes for the Republicans in the Spanish Civil War, and fought in Europe with anti-Fascists during World War II. This excerpt is from his novel The Conquerors *(1929), which details a Chinese uprising.*

glittering electric lights indicate the outlines of Chinese restaurants. Above them towers the mass of the famous, the formidable rock, wide-spreading at the base, gradually tapering into a double oriental boss, veiled with a light mist, and seeming to end in the stars. It does not give one the impression of a silhouette, or of a surface cut out in paper, but rather of something deep and solid, something like a black world. A line of lights (is it a road?) encircles the highest of the bosses, the Peak, like a necklace. The houses appear like a handful of lights incredibly close to one another, almost on the top of the twinkling outline of Chinese restaurants, dwindling like the rock as it ascends, until it is lost among the more substantial stars. In the bay are numerous steamboats, at anchor, with their storeys of portholes shedding zigzag lights, which mingle with those of the town. All these lights in Chinese skies and waters do not suggest the power of the whites who made them, but rather some Polynesian scene, one of those feasts in which painted gods are honoured by the scattering of clouds of glow-worms into the darkness. . . .

Then there passes before us an indistinct screen, hiding everything, its only sound that of a one-stringed guitar. It is a junk. The air is warm and still. . . .

Wang Tao

MY SOJOURN IN HONG KONG

THE AFTERNOON OF the next day I arrived in Hong Kong. The hills all around are rather bare of trees, and nothing but water meets the eyes. The people appear rather stupid and speak a dialect that is quite unintelligible. The experience was so exasperating when I first arrived that I felt that I could hardly stand it.

My residence was halfway up the mountain, surrounded

Wang Tao was radical for a nineteenth-century Chinese scholar: he strongly advocated the study of Western literature. Eventually, Tao's free-thinking got him into hot water. In 1880, after his connections with the Taiping Rebellion were unearthed, he was kicked out of China—all the way to Hong Kong.

by banyans. Several large plantain trees could be seen outside the window, greeting the eyes with their luscious green. In the evening I was just dashing off a letter to my family by lamplight when the sound of a Chinese fiddle arose in the neighbourhood. Someone was singing sonorously to the accompaniment of the instrument. The sound of music in a foreign place only makes one sad.

Hong Kong was originally a barren isle. There is very little flat land between the mountains and the sea, perhaps a few yards altogether. Here the Europeans have made painstaking efforts in planning and building. Their persistence reminds one of the mythical *jingwei* bird that endeavoured to fill up the sea with pebbles, and the "foolish old man" who tried to move mountains. Land in this area is now so costly that even a few square feet can command a fantastic price.

The district near the shore is the commercial district. It is divided into three so-called "rings," the "Upper," "Central" and "Lower" Rings, named in accordance with the topographical features of the hillside. Later, another

Ring was added, so there are now four of them. The local people often refer to this last Ring as the "Apron-string Road," an appellation which evidently derived from the way it circuits the hillside.

The people of Guangdong province have always had something of a monopoly on commerce, and thus Hong Kong has proved to be attractive to craftsmen from far and wide. Business flourishes here, and trade relations have been established with many places.

The people of Hong Kong depend mainly on mountain springs for their drinking water, which is pure and refreshing. Chickens and pigs are inexpensive, but are not as delicious as those from Jiangsu and Zhejiang provinces. The ocean fish have a pronounced fishy flavour. Most fresh-water fish come from Guangzhou, but cannot be kept for very long.

The streets in the Upper and Central Rings are closely lined with imposing shops. Passers-by are so numerous that they are constantly jostling against each other, and it is both noisy and dusty. The Lower Ring, by contrast, is more tranquil and shady, with plenty of trees. It is less densely populated and retains a rural atmosphere. Many Europeans have built their summer houses in the district known as Pokfulam. This picturesque neighbourhood is a fit place for those who seek solitude and relaxation. The district beyond the Lower Ring is mostly inhabited by the fishermen, many of whom spend their entire lives on boats.

Central Ring has St. Paul's College, and Ying Wah College stands at the junction of Upper and Lower Rings. Great College is located in Upper Ring. In all these institutions students are taught Western languages so that they can render useful service to the government upon graduation. Ying Wah College has an automated typesetting machine and printing facilities.

The highest point of Upper Ring is Tai Ping Shan. Here the streets are neatly lined on both sides with gaudy houses sporting brightly painted doors and windows hung with fancy curtains. These are the brothels, which are literally packed with singsong girls. It is a pity that most of them have large natural feet, and that those with tiny

One place of abiding interest near my home is the museum, which houses a large collection of books in European languages. Everyone is free to go in and read them. The books cover numerous subjects, including geography, anatomy and mechanics, and all contain detailed illustrations. In the courtyard there is a display of specimens of various kinds of birds, fish, animals, plants, and trees. They are so finely preserved that that they appear to be alive.

Next to the museum stands the opera house, where the Europeans go for plays and concerts. Among the performances, magicians occupy a prominent place. Their skills are very great indeed, often achieving feats which seem incredible.

The British have set up three colleges. They are the St. Paul's College headed by Mr. Sung Mei, the Ying Wah College headed by Mr. James Legge and the "Great Britain College" headed by Mr. Shi An. These institutions only admit youths of departments, while the rest will be recommended to other establishments.

Near St. Paul's College and the City Hall, there is a tract of wooded land with clumps of bamboo and carpet-like lawns under lofty trees. I have taken many a pleasant stroll there at sunset. When the refreshing breeze blows through my sleeves, I often feel a strong reluctance to turn back.

The buildings in the Central Ring are particularly magnificent, and many are veritable mansions. This is the principal commercial district. The streets are broader, too. Therefore, it is not as noisy and chaotic as Upper Ring.

There is a huge striking clock near the water's edge. When it strikes the hours, it can be heard at a distance of several miles.

Pokfulam, where the Europeans have their summer houses, is rather distant from where I live. Handsome villas equipped with all sorts of conveniences have been built there in great numbers. They are set in picturesque surroundings, with lofty trees and flowering plants all around. The courtyards of many houses boast gurgling fountains. Sitting in the cool comfort of the airy rooms of such residences, one can almost forget the sultry summer weather. In such places, the cold drinks or iced fruit and melons so popular in summer seem quite unnecessary.

When Mr. Legge is not busy teaching, he sometimes invites me to spend a day in his Pokfulam home, where we while away the hours together reading or composing poems in the wafting breezes. Even immortals could hardly aspire to such pleasure. I owe it to Mr. Legge's unstinting friendship that I am allowed to share his comfort in the hot season.

A short walk away from where Mr. Legge resides, there is a reservoir—a broad expanse of calm water, so lucid that one can see right to the bottom. There is a guards' lodge nearby, for the reservoir is watched by sentries to prevent the water from being poisoned. The people of Hong Kong depend primarily on that reservoir for drinking water. The supply never stops even in the dry season. This is indeed a great boon.

The villas owned by European merchants at Pokfulam have been built in a variety of styles and are reached by flights of stairs. Many are surrounded by high walls topped by battlements; it is as if their proprietors were prepared to defend themselves against attack from hostile countries. Europeans are always on the alert, and arm themselves even at home. Their houses are built on hillsides or mountain tops, and command magnificent views. The sea stretches out before you all the way to the endless horizon; vast networks of mountains appear like little mounds. Ships and boats of every description lie at anchor in neat rows in the harbour, which appears no larger than a spittoon. Such sights are a delight to the eye as well as the mind.

Some of the houses are built in Japanese style, complete with bamboo screens and paper windows. They are remarkable for their cleanliness and refinement.

In the past the island of Hong Kong was free of mosquitoes. However, the planting of many trees and plants has led to a serious infestation of these insects. The way they frequently disturb one's sleep is one of the major drawbacks of the place.

By following a tortuous path, one will eventually reach the Peak. There is a tiny hut perched there which serves as a lodge for the guards, with a tall flagpole standing beside it. When a ship arrives from a foreign port, a flag will be hoisted to inform the people who live further down the hill of its arrival. I have climbed up there, and standing in the wind, dropped my handkerchief, only to have it fly back to me. The guard told me, "The wind always blows towards the summit." This phenomenon is hard to explain.

Visitors from distant places generally lodge in the guest houses. These consist of a number of buildings large and small that are spread out over an area of several acres planted with lovely flowers and shrubs. However, there are no pavilions and pagodas here. In this respect, they are inferior to the mansions of China. At sunset when the moon comes out, many distinguished Europeans gather here to enjoy the cool breezes. Dressed in their finest, they stand together chatting in small groups, or stroll leisurely through the grounds in pairs. The scene gives one the impression that these people are thoroughly enjoying themselves on their sojourn in a foreign place.

During my stay in Hong Kong, I worked together with Dr. Legge on the translation of *The Thirteen Classics*. Before he was called back to Britain, he discussed the possibility of my going to Europe to assist him with further translations. In the winter of 1867, I received a letter from. him inviting me there, and made up my mind to take the trip. My friends in Hong Kong arranged a farewell dinner in my honour at the Apricot Blossom Restaurant. We all enjoyed ourselves immensely chatting over our cups. Then on 20 October I boarded a foreign ship which departed promptly at ten o'clock in the morning.

Jan Morris

HONG KONG

HONG KONG IS in China, if not entirely of it, and after nearly 150 years of British rule the background to all its wonders remains its Chineseness—98 percent if you reckon it by population, hardly less if you are thinking metaphysically.

It may not look like it from the deck of an arriving ship, or swooping into town on a jet, but geographically

Novelist and essayist Jan Morris is renowned for her travel writing, which has appeared in numerous magazines and is collected in six books. This excerpt is from one of her most popular works, Hong Kong *(1985). Morris lives in Wales.*

most of the territory is rural China still. The empty hills that form the mass of the New Territories, the precipitous islets and rocks, even some of the bare slopes of Hong Kong Island itself, rising directly above the tumultuous harbor, are much as they were in the days of the Manchus, the Mings or the neolithic Yaos. The last of the leopards has indeed been shot (1931), the last of the tigers spotted (1967, it is claimed), but that recondite newt flourishes still as *Paramesotriton hongkongensis*, there are still civets, pythons, barking deer and porcupines about and the marshlands abound with seabirds. The predominant country colors are Chinese colors, browns, grays, tawny colors. The generally opaque light is just the light one expects of China, and gives the whole territory the required suggestion of blur, surprise and uncertainty. The very smells are Chinese smells—oily, laced with duck-mess and gasoline.

Thousands of Hong Kong people still live on board junks, cooking their meals in the hiss and flicker of pressure lamps among the riggings and the nets.

Thousands more inhabit shantytowns, made of sticks, canvas and corrugated iron but bustling with the native vivacity. People are still growing fruit, breeding fish, running duck farms, tending oyster beds; a few still grow rice and a very few still plow their fields with water buffalo. Village life remains resiliently ancestral. The Tangs and the Pangs are influential. The geomancers are busy still. Half-moon graves speckle the high ground wherever *feng shui* decrees, sometimes attended still by the tall brown urns that contain family ashes. Temples to Tin Hau, the Queen of Heaven, or Hung Shing, God of the Southern Seas, still stand incense-swirled upon foreshores.

But the vast majority of Hong Kong's Chinese citizens live in towns, jam-packed on the flatter ground. They are mostly squeezed in gigantic tower-blocks, and they have surrounded themselves with all the standard manifestations of modern non-Communist chinoiserie: the garish merry signs, the clamorous shop-fronts, the thickets of TV aerials, the banners, the rows of shiny hanging ducks, the washing on its poles, the wavering bicycles, the potted plants massed on balconies, the canvas-canopied stalls selling herbs, or kitchenware, or antiques, or fruit, the bubbling caldrons of crab-claw soup boiling at eating stalls, the fantastic crimson-and-gold facades of restaurants, the flickering television screens in shop windows, the trays of sticky cakes in confectionery stores, the profusion of masts, poles and placards protruding from the fronts of buildings, the dragons carved or gilded, the huge elaborate posters, the tea shops with their gleaming pots, the smells of cooking, spice, incense, oil, the racket of radio music and amplified voices, the half-shouted conversation that is peculiar to Chinese meeting one another in the street, the ceaseless clatter of spoons, coins, mah-jongg counters, abaci, hammers and electric drills.

It can appear exotic to visitors, but it is fundamentally a plain and practical style. Just as the Chinese consider a satisfactory year to be a year in which nothing much happens, so their genius seems to me fundamentally of a workaday kind, providing a stout and reliable foundation, mat and bamboo, so to speak, on which to build the structures of astonishment.

WHAT THE WEST has provided, originally through the medium of the British Empire, later by the agency of international finance, is a city-state in its own image, overlaying that resilient and homely Chinese style with an aesthetic far more aggressive. The capitalists of Hong Kong have been terrific builders, and have made of the great port, its hills and its harbors, one of the most thrilling of all metropolitan prospects—for my own tastes, the finest sight in Asia. More than 5.5 million people, nearly twice the population of New Zealand, live here in less than four hundred square miles of land, at least half of which is rough mountain country. They are necessarily packed tight, in urban forms as startling in the luminous light of Hong Kong as the upper-works of the clippers must have been when they first appeared along its waterways.

The Tangs and the Lius may still be in their villages, but they are invested on all sides by massive New Towns, started from scratch in starkly modernist manner. All over the mainland New Territories, wherever the hills allow, busy roads sweep here and there, clumps of tower-blocks punctuate the skyline, suburban estates develop and blue-tiled brick wilts before the advance of concrete. Even on the outlying islands, as Hong Kong calls the rest of the archipelago, apartment buildings and power stations rise above the moors. Flatland in most parts of Hong Kong being so hard to find, this dynamic urbanism has been created largely in linear patterns, weaving along shorelines, clambering up gullys or through narrow passes, and frequently compressed into almost inconceivable congestion. Some 80 percent of the people live in 8 percent of the land, and parts of Kowloon, with more than a quarter of a million people per square mile, are probably the most crowded places in all human history. An amazing tangle of streets complicates the topography; the architect I. M. Pei, commissioned to design a new Hong Kong office block in the 1980s, said it took nine months just to figure out access to the site.

There is not much shape to all this, except the shape of the place itself. Twin cities of the harbor are the vortex of all Hong Kong, and all that many strangers ever see of it. On the north, the mainland shore, the dense complex of districts called Kowloon presses away into the hills, projecting its force clean through them indeed by tunnel into the New Territories beyond. The southern shore, on the island of Hong Kong proper, is the site of the original British settlement, officially called Victoria but now usually known simply as Central; it is in effect the capital of Hong Kong, and contains most of its chief institutions, but it straggles inchoately all along the island's northern edge, following the track worn by the junk crews when, before the British came at all, adverse winds obliged them to drag their vessels through this strait. Around the two conglomerates the territory's being revolves: one talks of Kowloon-side or Hong Kong-side, and on an average day in 1987 more than 115,000 vehicles passed through the underwater tunnel from one to the other.

Once the colony had a formal urban center. Sit with me now in the Botanical Gardens, those inescapable amenities of the British Empire that have defied progress even here, and still provide shady boulevards, flower beds and a no more than usually nasty little zoo almost in the heart of Central. From this belvedere, fifty years ago, we could have looked down upon a ceremonial plaza of some dignity, Statue Square. It opened directly upon the harbor, rather like the Piazza d'Italia in Trieste, and to the west ran a waterfront esplanade, called the Praya after its Macao original. The steep green island hills rose directly behind the square, and it was surrounded by structures of consequence—Government House, where the Governor lived; Head Quarter House, where the General lived; a nobly classical City Hall; the Anglican cathedral; the Supreme Court; the Hongkong and Shanghai Bank. The effect was sealed by the spectacle of the ships passing to and fro at the north end of the square, and by the presence of four emblematically imperial prerequisites: a dockyard of the Royal Navy, a cricket field, the Hong Kong Club and a statue of Queen Victoria.

It has all been thrown away. Today Statue Square is blocked altogether out of our sight by office buildings, and anyway only the specter of a plaza remains down there, loomed over, fragmented by commercialism. Even the waterfront has been pushed back by land reclamation. The surviving promenade is all bits and pieces of piers, and a three-story car park obstructs the harbor view. The cricket ground has been prettified into a municipal garden, with turtles in a pond. Government House and the cathedral are hardly visible through the skyscrapers, the Hong Kong Club occupies four floors of a twenty-four-story office block. Queen Victoria has gone.

This is the way of urban Hong Kong. It is cramped by the force of nature, but it is irresistibly restless by instinct. Except for the harbor, it possesses no real center now. As we shall later see, the territory as a whole has lately become a stupendous exercise in social design, but no master plan for the harbor cities has ever succeeded— Sir Patrick Abercrombie offered one in the heyday of British town planning after the Second World War, but like so many of his schemes it never came to anything. Proposals to extend that promenade were repeatedly frustrated down the years, notably by the military, who would not get their barracks and dockyards out of the way; all that is left of the idea is the howling expressway that runs on stilts along the foreshore.

Today beyond Statue Square, all along the shoreline, across the harbor, far up the mountain slopes, tall concrete buildings extend without evident pattern or logic. There seems to be no perspective to them either, so that when we shift our viewpoint one building does not move with any grace against another—just a clump here, a splodge there, sometimes a solitary pillar of glass or concrete. Across the water they loom monotonously behind the Kowloon waterfront, square and Stalinesque; they are limited to a height of twelve stories there, because the airport is nearby. On the sides of distant mountains you may see them protruding from declining ridges like sudden outcrops of white chalk. Many are still meshed in bamboo scaffolding, many more are doomed to imminent demolition. If we look down the hill again, behind the poor governor's palace immolated in its gardens, we may see the encampment of blue-and-white awnings, interspersed with bulldozers and scattered with the laboring straw-hatted figures of construction workers, which shows where the foundations of yet another skyscraper, still bigger, more splendid and more extravagant no doubt than the one before, are even now being laid.

IF THERE IS no civic diagram to Hong Kong, no more is there a Hong Kong style of architecture—even the standard forms of Britain's Eastern empire found only precarious footholds in this colony. The old Chinese buildings here and there are, for the most part, just old Chinese buildings, while except for a few recent surprises the Euro-American blocks are standard modernist mediocrity.

The British first raised the flat at the northwestern end of Hong Kong Island, at a spot they called Possession Point. Today it is well inland, and is occupied by indeterminate Chinese tenements, apartment houses and offices, with no plaque to mark the spot, only the name Possession Street on a lane nearby. Somewhere here, we may assume, the colonists put up their first temporary buildings—the shanties that are still called in Hong Kong mat-sheds, walled with bamboo poles and roofed with matting. The first permanent European building in Hong Kong, however, was very properly a granite warehouse built without official permission by Jardine, Matheson, while the first proper European house was James Matheson's veranda'ed bungalow nearby, cattily described at the time as being "half New South Wales, half native production," and surrounded by a plantation of sickly coconuts.

Presently buildings went up in a neo-Mediterranean mode copied from Macao. Along the island waterfront rose offices and warehouses with tiled roofs and arcades, awnings and jalousies, which, becoming fretted and peeling as the years passed, at least give the place an authentically hot-weather look. The traveler Isabella Bird, in 1879, thought it looked like Genoa. The young

Kipling, arriving ten years later, was reminded of the Calcutta style. Very few of these buildings are left intact, but embedded among the tower-blocks one may sometimes see the half-blocked remains of a colonnade, with balconied windows above it, perhaps, as of a piano nobile, and sagging jalousies.

The later Victorians built Victorianly, regardless in their confident way of climate or precedent. They built some grandiosely classical buildings, and some engaging examples, with balustrades and pointed arches, of the style they used to call Indo-Saracenic. They erected no prodigies in Hong Kong, like their masterpieces in India, but for a time they did give the place some monumentalism. The buildings around Statue Square, the shipping offices with their tiers of Venetian arches, the pompous banks, the properly Gothic university—when the globe-trotters of fin-de-siècle sailed into Hong Kong these buildings made them feel they were entering an outpost of the great imperial order. "A little England in the eastern seas," dutifully but unconvincingly wrote the future King George V, at the instruction of his tutor, when with his brother Eddy he visited Hong Kong in 1881.

But it never acquired majesty, or real elegance, or cohesion, or even an assured identity. A reporter for the *Illustrated London News,* surveying the Anglican cathedral when it first went up, called it "an unsightly pile, quite disturbing the oriental appearance of the place," while *The Encyclopedia of the British Empire,* c.1900, remarked cooly that "the architecture of Hong Kong is of a somewhat mixed character." Mixed it has decidedly remained, and a tragic lesson in wasted opportunity—for what a miraculous city could have been built upon this site, backed by hill and island, fronted by the China seas! Too late: as it approaches its end as a city-state Hong Kong is more than ever a topographical marvel, an architectural hodgepodge.

THE FUNDAMENTALS, THEN, are plain and practical, the design is inchoate, the architecture of a somewhat mixed character; yet Hong Kong is astonishingly beautiful. It is made so partly by its setting, land and sea so exquisitely interacting, but chiefly by its impression of irresistible activity. It is like a caldron, seething, hissing, hooting, arguing, enmeshed in a labyrinth of tunnels and overpasses, with those skyscrapers erupting everywhere into view, with ferries churning and hovercraft splashing and great jets flying in, with fleets of ships lying always offshore, with double-decker buses and clinging tramcars, with a car it seems for every square foot of roadway, with a pedestrian for every inch of sidewalk, and funicular trains crawling up and down the mountainside, and small scrubbed-faced policemen scudding about on motorbikes—all in all, with a pace of life so unremitting, a sense of movement and enterprise so challenging, that one's senses are overwhelmed by the sheer glory of human animation.

Or perhaps by the power of human avarice. The beauty is the beauty, like it or not, of the capitalist system. More than a usual share of this city's energies goes towards the making of money, and nobody has ever pretended otherwise: as a *Hong Kong Weekly* writer calling herself "Veronica" frankly put it in 1907, in this colony "plenty of money and plenty of push will always ensure you a seat in High Places, supposing you are desirous of the same." It was the prospect of wealth, more than the exertion of pride or power, that brought the British here in the first place, in a classic reversal of the dictum that trade follows the flag. Even in times when evangelical improvement was a powerful motive of imperialism the merchants of Hong Kong abided by the principles of *laissez-faire* at their most conscienceless—"We have every respect," as James Matheson himself wrote, "for persons entertaining strict religious principles, but we fear that very godly people are not suited to the drug trade."

Today only a solitary bronze financier stands in Statue Square, but even in the prime of Empire, when Queen Victoria was still on her plinth and the offices of Authority stood lordly all around, the most imposing of the central buildings were those of the Hongkong and Shanghai Bank, the Chartered Bank next door and the Hong Kong Club, storied stronghold of the business classes. The merchants and financiers have always aspired to be top dogs in this city, and have never been afraid to show it, in a conceit that is notorious, a histrionic flair and a legendary hospitality to strangers. James Pope-Hennessy, writing about Hong Kong in the 1960s, waspishly dubbed it Half-Crown Colony, and used as a test for his books the one famous poem ever written in English about the place, W. H. Auden's "Hong Kong":

> Its leading characters are wise and witty,
> Their suits well-tailored, and they wear them well,
> Have many a polished parable to tell
> About the mores of a trading city.

> Only the servants enter unexpected,
> Their silent movements make dramatic news;
> Here in the East our bankers have erected
> A worthy temple to the Comic Muse.

TO THE COMIC muse perhaps, at least in the eyes of iconoclastic 1930s poets, but to the epic muse too, for

there has frequently been something heroic to the ostenta-
tion of Hong Kong. In its early days the crews of Hong
Kong clippers earned far more than other sailors, and
splendidly proclaimed the fact in the polish, the gleaming
paintwork, the scrub-white decks and elaborate decoration
of their ships. Today's rich are much the same, and as a
matter of fact the wealth is remarkably widely distributed.
Its impact upon the temper of the place is by no means
confined to the business center and the expensive residen-
tial areas, where the prevalence of high finance sometimes
makes everything feel like Conglomerate City, an international settlement of the plutocracy. On the contrary, a
sense of satisfied avarice is pervasive nearly everywhere,
because almost everybody makes *more* money here: the
Chinese taxi driver gets far more than his comrade in
Guangzhou, the Australian journalist makes far more that
his colleagues in Sydney. Chinese dollar-millionaires,
though difficult to pin down, can certainly be numbered
in the scores of thousands, while a foreigner can spend a
few years in Hong Kong and retire home rich—in 1987 a

British lawyer threw a party to celebrate the earning of his first £1 million from a single protracted court case.

The most showy of the plutocrats are the Chinese. That pink Rolls-Royce could only belong to a Chinese magnate. That young man so loudly quoting multidigit investment terms over his cellular telephone in the coffee shop is inevitably a Chinese broker. Chinese tycoons own all the most exuberantly exhibitionist of the mansions, the ones with the palace gardens, the ceremonial gateways and the great red dragon sentinels. But irrespective of race a deliberate display of wealth characterizes all of the upper ranks of the business community, and unavoidably affects the general atmosphere.

For example every Sunday morning you may see, bobbing offshore beside Queen's Pier at Central, or in the harbor at Aberdeen on the island's southern coast, the launches, yachts and shiny motorized junks that take the well-off to their Sabbath pleasures. Some fly the flags of great banks or merchant companies, some belong to lesser concerns—even law partnerships maintain pleasure-junks in Hong Kong. Some are just family craft, or love boats. Whatever their ownership, they are likely to have trimly uniformed Chinese boat crews, and awnings over their high poops, and probably white-clothed tables already laid with bottles, coolers and cutlery. Off they go, one after another, towing speedboats sometimes, with laughter ringing out across the water. Girls are stretched out for sunbathing on the prow, owners in blazers and white slacks are already sharing a first Buck's Fizz with their guests, who are very likely visitors from overseas, and look at once jet-lagged, red-faced from the sun and elated by the lavishness of it all.

The rich of Hong Kong, if they do not live in plush apartments, tend to live in Marbellan or Hollywoodian kinds of houses, all marble pools and patios on hillsides, and love to show themselves at public occasions—looking bronzed and well-diamonded at cocktail parties, vulgarly furred at the races (Hong Kong shamelessly declares itself the fur-buying capital of the world), bidding effervescently at charity auctions or most characteristically of all, perhaps, sailing into the Sunday morning on those yachts and varnished junks. All this is faithfully recorded in the pages of the *Hong Kong Tatler,* which supplements its portraits of successful financiers, and its property pages advertising attractive well-converted farmhouses in the vicinity of Grasse or fabulous golfing environments on the coast of southern Spain, with copiously illustrated reports of the social goings-on.

I thumb my way through a few typical issues of the late 1980s. Dr. and Mrs. Henry Li, Sir Y. K. Pao, Lady Kadoorie, Mr. Simon Keswick and Mr. Hu Fa-Kuang celebrate the recent elevation of the Hon. H. M. G. Forsgate to his Commandership of the Order of the British Empire. Mr. Stanley Ho, Mr. Teddy Yip and Dr. Nuno da Cunha e Tavora Forena welcome Dr. Henry Kissinger to a dinner party. Who are these lovely people enjoying their drinks aboard the yacht *Bengal I*? Why, they are members of the 100 Elite of Hong Kong, the magazines says, being entertained by the Japanese billionaire Masakazu Kobayashi on Repulse Bay. "He came, he saw, he cocktailed," quips the *Tatler* of a visit by the Chinese People's Republic director of Hong Kong Affairs, and here he is doing it, wearing a very large boutonniere. M. and Mme. François Heriard-Debreuil, of Rémy-Martin cognac, present the Rémy X.O. Cup to Mr. Wong Kwoon Chung and his fellow owners of Champion Joker (trainer Kau Ping Chi, jockey B. Raymond): and sure enough, here on a back page associates of Beresford Cresvale (Far East), enjoying a party aboard the brigantine *Wan Fu,* are to be seen upon the quarterdeck toasting the world with frosted drinks in the sunshine.

There are always visiting swells to grace these occasions. To many fashionable transients Hong Kong is hardly more than a distant extension of the New York-London-Paris round of profitable socializing, and everyone grand and famous comes to Hong Kong at one time or another. I was once strolling in the Botanical Gardens when Bernhard, Prince of the Netherlands, appeared with a brisk retinue of courtiers, all of whom looked like elderly English colonels in a British movie of the Second World War. Startled by their sudden arrival, and not at first recognizing the royal features, I stopped dead in my tracks and demanded of this impressive brigade who they all were; but they took me for an Extremist, and hurried by.

OF COURSE IT is not all pleasure—it soon becomes apparent to the stranger that few smart events in Hong Kong are pure pleasure. They are nearly always viewed with an eye to the main chance, and in fact half the parties recorded in the *Tatler* are really commercial functions, to woo clients, to cherish business associations or even frankly to plug a product. Business life is a gamble, and both the British and the Chinese have always enjoyed gambling (the Chinese used to run books on competing candidates for the Imperial Civil Service examinations); so since the early days of the Crown Colony one of the chief places for combining business with pleasure, and thus exhibiting the plutocratic style of Hong Kong, has been the racecourse.

Since 1871 gambling in the colony has been legal only if you are gambling on horses. The Chinese have always

assiduously evaded this puritanical decree, betting incessantly on mah-jongg behind closed doors, crossing the
border to clubs and casinos in more tolerant places—in
former times to Kowloon City or the village of Shenzhen
across the Chinese border on the mainland, nowadays to
Macao, whose casinos are Hong Kong–owned. They will
gamble on anything, and are obsessed with omens and
numbers; rich Chinese will happily pay HK$250,000 for
lucky car numbers, when the government auctions them
for charity.

And Ring-a-Rolls will send you, if you ask them, a
lucky-numbered Silver Shadow or Silver Spur to take you
to the Happy Valley racecourse on Saturday afternoon—
even the price, HK$668, will be in well-omened digits,
both double sixes and eights being famously propitious.
Several million citizens would rent one, if they could
afford it, for the races grip the Hong Kong masses as
nothing else: when, in 1986, three hundred detectives in
forty squads simultaneously cracked down on drug traf-
fickers and loan sharks all over the territory, they chose

that moment of universal distraction, the start of the three o'clock race at Happy Valley.

The course is almost as old as Hong Kong itself. It occupies a valley in the island hills which the early settlers thought especially desirable, but which was later found to be unhealthy for European residence and reserved instead for recreation (and for burial, in cemeteries on the slopes around). There is a second racecourse now at Shatin in the New Territories, but Happy Valley, still overlooked by its burial grounds, remains the headquarters of the Royal Hong Kong Jockey Club and thus one of the symbolical assembly points of Hong Kong.

They used to say that the colony was ruled by the Jockey Club, the Hong Kong and Shanghai Bank and the Governor, and the club remains immensely influential still. Its twelve stewards invariably include leading members of the old British merchant companies, who have been racing their ponies and horses at this track for 140 years, and representatives of the newer but equally powerful Chinese plutocracy. Its secretary nowadays is usually a retired

British general. Legally the Jockey Club is obliged to hand over its profits to charitable purposes: it largely paid for the Hong Kong Polytechnic, and all over Hong Kong you may see clinics, schools and other worthy bodies financed by its totalizers.

But Happy Valley on race day (twice a week throughout the season) does not feel like a charitable place. For a start its arrangements are exceedingly lavish. Even the horses at their training stables beyond the course have air-conditioned quarters and swimming pools. In the middle of the track a vast video screen shows the whole of every race, so that no punter need miss a single foot of the action, and throughout the grandstands computers are clicking and screens are flashing. Nothing feels cheap or makeshift, and this is only proper, for I have been told that as much money is often laid during an afternoon at Happy Valley as is staked on one day in all the race-courses of England put together.

The Jockey Club's own premises are very splendid. Up in a hushed elevator one goes, and on every floor there seems to be a different restaurant—each with a different name, each jam-packed with racegoers Chinese and European, scoffing *coq au vin* with Chambertin in one, bird's-nest soup with brandy at another, while keeping watchful eyes flickering between race cards and the closed-circuit TV screens dotted around the walls. Hong Kong's palpable aura of money is everywhere—scented as always with perfumes, cigar smoke and the smells of rich food, and accentuated by the small groups of men who, standing aside from the bars and restaurants, are here and there to be seen deep in distinctly unfrivolous (and patently uncharitable) conversation.

Other clubs have their own quarters in the stands—the Hong Kong Club, the American Club, the Lusitano Club—and high above it all are the private boxes of the very, very influential, where the greatest merchants and their guests, a visiting senator from the United States perhaps, a TV star from London, a couple of Italian tycoons, some Japanese bankers and a Scottish earl eat magnificent luncheons, discuss terms, conclude deals, swap innuendos, savor nuances and adjourn now and then to watch the races in an atmosphere of impregnable exclusivity, heightened into excitement partly by alcohol, partly by the prevailing sense of power. Once I lunched myself in such a box, feeling shamelessly privileged; more often I have glimpsed these occasions through half-open doors, as I have prowled the corridors outside, and this is a far more suggestive experience.

Like Hong Kong itself, Happy Valley on race day is a bitter, brilliant, grasping place, not in the least blasé or world-weary. The tensions that grip any racecourse towards the end of a race seems to affect Happy Valley with an extra *frisson,* sweeping through the stands like a gale out of the hills. The Chinese proletariat below may take it stoically, and the rich Chinese above them, too, preserve for the most part their smooth self-control, but the Europeans are different: eminent financiers and women in silks leap to their feet with the thrill of a finish, the men shouting meaningless exhortations like "Come on, Champion Joker," the women sometimes jumping up and down like participants in an American TV quiz.

It is a curious spectacle, in a city that spends all its working days so assiduously in pursuit of profit—who would think a casual bet could mean so much?—and it leaves in more dilettante minds a disturbingly fanatic impression. If you are of this temperament, better not look through your binoculars at the faces of the winning owners or the successful trainer when the victorious horse is led into the ring below, and the big gold cup is presented—occasionally one can get a nasty shock, from the malevolent satisfaction their expressions seem to convey, as they look triumphantly round them at their rivals.

AS I WRITE there is a Chinese living on the sidewalk at Sung Wang Toi Road, near the airport. Everyone in the neighborhood knows him, a tall, very brown, handsome but emaciated man with a short black beard and a high forehead, always carrying a stick, who strides incessantly around his patch of pavement with a stylish strut.

His name is Tse Pui-ying, and he is mad. Everyone knows him, but nobody can get near him—make the slightest attempt to approach and he will threaten you with his stick, swear at you, or throw stones. He has no identity card, he has no address. He spends all his days scavenging the gutters for food, and watching the aircraft come and go deafeningly above his head.

He is one poor citizen alienated forever, from his kind and from his own humanity, by the relentless personality of Hong Kong. Another was the wife of an itinerant goldfish hawker who briefly entered into the news when, faced with imminent eviction from her miserable tenement flat, suffering from protracted postnatal depression and the aftermath of an abortion, she hanged her two children, cut her own wrists and jumped to her death from a fifth-floor window.

There are days when I feel that it is all too much, that the place has become a cruel parody of itself. The day of the woman's death was one, and another occurred less heartrendingly soon afterwards, when two items dom-

inated the local news. First Mr. Rupert Murdoch, con-
troller of newspapers, magazines, television and radio stations throughout the world, bought what would soon
develop into control of the *South China Morning Post,* "the
most profitable newspaper company in the world, using
the world's most modern computer system"——for in
Hong Kong, sagely observed the *Post* itself, "everything is
for sale . . . everything has its price." Then the daughter
of the chairman of the Hongkong and Shanghai Bank
married an Australian theater manager at the Cathedral of
the Immaculate Conception, and all the rich of Hong
Kong, all the powerful, all the fashionable ("government
officials, judges, business leaders and other celebrities")
were driven beflowered and gray-toppered in mini-buses
to a reception at Skyhigh, the chairman's residence on a
high pinnacle of the Peak, which has a gatehouse like a
Spanish castle, and can be seen like a fortress from far
away. Thrust into obscurer columns by these great events
were all the everyday occurrences and preoccupations of
the city-state, the suicides, the pitiful petty crimes, the

seizures of smuggled heroin, the scandals about insurance rates or housing conditions, the sad prevalence of traffic accidents at Tuen Mun, the debates about 1997. . . .

These are familiar provocations of Hong Kong, which has repelled visiting liberals for generations. Successions of reformers have sought to disturb the conscience of the world, and especially of the British, about the state of this colony—about its reactionary political system, its social inequities and its unlovely motives. Everyone feels that way sometimes—there are far more compassionate people in Hong Kong than you might guess from first impressions—and nearly everyone is intermittently chilled by the contrast between the splendors of mansions like Skyhigh, the spilling of money by billionaires, and the hardships of Hong Kong's poor living in such fantastic congestion down the hill.

It is an abnormal city. Until our own times it has been predominantly a city of refugees, with all the hallmarks of a refugee society—the single-minded obsession with the making of money, amounting almost to neurosis, and the perpetual sense of underlying insecurity, which makes everything more tense and more nervous. Only recently, as we shall presently discover, has the emergence of a new, educated Chinese middle class, born and bred in the colony, made one feel that Hong Kong is approaching some kind of social equilibrium, becoming a real, balanced city—and with 1997 closing fast, perhaps it is too late.

Yet for myself I find that in a place where for so long almost everyone, rich or poor, of every age and every race, has been frankly out for the main chance, a curious sense of liberation obtains. Hong Kong is not a place of pathos, not perhaps the right environment for very godly people. It has always been the brazen embodiment of free enterprise, or as a government official put it to me in the 1970s, of "Victorian economic principles, the only ones that have ever really worked." "We are just simple traders," said Sir Alexander Grantham, Governor of Hong Kong from 1947 to 1957, "who want to get on with our daily round and common task. This may not be very noble, but at any rate it does not disturb others." Nevertheless the foreigner's first response to this territory, Dr. McCoy's phase of euphoria, is justified. There are few places in the world where such a large proportion of the population is at least doing what it wants to do, where it wants to be, and in a poll of Chinese residents in 1982 only 2 percent admitted to any "unmitigated dislike" of Hong Kong. I would have been among the 2 percent myself then, but the years have changed my responses.

Sometimes in the early evening I like to walk down to one of the city waterfronts, to watch the lights of the ships go by, share the pleasures of the couples strolling along the piers, or eat fried chicken on a bench in the gathering dark. The air is likely to be rich and humid, the sky is lit with the brooding glow of a great city's lights, blotting out the stars. It does not matter where I am, Kowloon or Hong Kong-side; around me always, beyond the little pool of quiet I have made for myself on bench or bollard, the huge endless stir of the place, the roar of the traffic, the passing of the ships, the comings and goings of the ferries, combine into one gigantic sensation of communal energy. For the most part, I know very well, it is not energy expended in any very high flown purpose, but still its ceaseless rumble and motion move me, and I sit there gnawing my chicken, drinking my San Miguel beer from the can, more or less entranced.

Among the mingled noises of the evening, one is generally inescapable, *thump, thump, thump,* somewhere or other along the waterfront, across the harbor, behind me in the recesses of the city or far away in the dark countryside beyond. It is the sound of a jackhammer, the leitmotif of Hong Kong. It may be helping to pull a building down, it may be putting another one up, and in one guise or another it has been dictating the impacts and images of the place since the first developers settled on this foreshore 150 years ago.

Lynn Pan

TRACING IT HOME

IT WAS THE death of my grandmother, quite literally.
I discovered how she died some time after my trip to
Shanghai. Before that it hadn't occurred to me to ask
about her, and in any case I had got into the habit of
never asking my father difficult questions. There were
hints at some unpleasantness, something more than one
would care to speak of, but it wasn't until I had a chance

*Lynn Pan was born in Shanghai and currently lives in Hong Kong. Her
previous five novels include* In Search of Old Shanghai *and* Gangsters
in Paradise. *Pan's latest book,* Tracing It Home: Journeys around a
Chinese Family (1992), *is a series of autobiographical tales, from which
this excerpt is taken.*

to talk to my father's sister, the aunt I call Niangniang, that I learned what exactly happened.

Niangniang lives in theory with a married daughter in Sydney. Finding Australia dull, she would pop up so frequently in Hong Kong that she'd end up maintaining a flat there. I, too, was often in Hong Kong in the years succeeding my trip to Shanghai, years of extensive travels in the Far East. And it was there, over dinner, that I made her tell me about my grandmother. I remember thinking, as she told me the story, I will always listen from now on, to aunts, uncles, father, to anyone who will tell me things.

In most people, memories are worn thin by time, or else they are silted over by the events and weariness of years; in Niangniang, though, the spool of threads joining her to the past was found, when pulled on, to be time-proof. Incident after incident lives on in her memory. Old wrongs that in others would have sunk into forgetfulness are living in her still. For her, the past is as real as the present and continues to happen, and this is not only because she is old, but because to many Chinese what happens in history is not past, but all part of their now (and in that sense, China may be said to have no history). What's more, her memory is of a different quality from Hanze's, less precise, more obsessive, brighter but also harsher in colour. You never feel with Niangniang that you are entering calmer waters, only more turbulent. What was felt, suffered, comes through: the lightness in the head, the clutch in the midriff.

That day, she quaffed Carlsbergs and rambled, mentioning names. One was of a man in Canton; him my interest homed on, because I myself was headed for that city the next day.

It was work which took me to Canton, but one thing I was never quite intent on doing in my one and a half days there was to look up this man Niangniang had mentioned. He is my father's half-brother, my grandfather's son by a mistress.

His mother was a woman of not entire virtue, called Bitao Laowu, Jade Peach Number Five. From the name most people in Shanghai would know that she was a singsong girl: that was the way they called them in the singsong house, Number So-and-so. As for the rest of her name, it was a sort of trademark; she was Jade Peach the way Clara Bow was the "It Girl" or Theda Bara "the Vamp."

I may mislead when I say "not entire virtue", because Jade Peach could very well have remained a virgin until she became my grandfather's mistress. She was alluring enough to be special, and special girls were saved up by the madams like treats. The exclusiveness of these girls was not only in their sexual immaculacy, but also in the fact that whoever paid for the privilege of deflowering one could, his means permitting, have her all to himself.

My grandmother knew all about Jade Peach, because after the affair had gone on for some time my grandfather had no qualms about bringing her home to tea occasionally.

To take this without a murmur was a lot to ask of any wife, even a Chinese one. What was more, though Jade Peach was the favorite she was not the only one. There was Miss Di, Pearl Number Six. Pearl had not quite Jade Peach's looks but she had more of the feminine wiles. They both, following custom, addressed my grandmother as "Sister", but the way she heard it they might have been saying "Ogre". I don't know how well Jade Peach and Pearl knew each other, or if they began their careers in the same establishment. Nor do I know to which of the six or seven grades of singsong girl they belonged—in other words, I don't know how high-class they were as courtesans. I always picture the ones at the top of the profession reclining on nests of brocade cushions and letting themselves get grossly fat from a combination of good living and boredom. I see creams and powders inside lacquered toilette boxes, and pairs of embroidered and beaded slippers under canopied beds. But I don't know if, where Jade Peach and Pearl were concerned, these images would serve.

My grandmother couldn't make a scene about these girls because her husband was apt to fly off the handle; once he threw a teapot at her. It was the tension in him, the edginess which came of always taking those tremendous risks in business. You couldn't really blame him if he was sometimes out of temper, and she didn't think she did; yet what else could it be but rage and reproach that she felt welling up inside her soul? There were occasions when she felt the day, the night, to be beyond the powers she had of living. There had been a few good years, at the beginning; but all good things must be paid for, either before or after.

From nobody might she expect sympathy, least of all from other women, who, after remarking, "Our kind know no choices," reckoned there was nothing more to be said. Who was she to think that better was due to her? It didn't do to think of the old times; instead, she should bow quietly to Fate. To that harem resignation one half of her assented, but with the other half she contemplated the alternative. She saw another course opening to her, that of sinking into nothingness. Only that, she saw, could put the torment behind her.

She knew what she must do. She waited till he was out one afternoon before she made for his opium couch. There was the drug, of a finer quality than which you would not easily find in Shanghai. You swallowed two lumps of it, raw. You washed it down with a cup of brandy, neat. And there you were, dead. After she had put the cup down she lay back in her bed and closed her eyes. Other women before her had come at last to this.

When they found her her brows were drawn clearly above the thin, smooth lids, and her hair, black and shiny, did not have a strand out of place. Her mouth was firmly closed, the lips bloodless. Her pulse still flickered, but would not do so for long. She was thirty-three years old; her son, my father, was four.

Both she and Jade Peach had had two sons by my grandfather, but just as Jade Peach had lost one of her

sons, so one of my grandmother's had died. No more
than eight months separated the birth of my father and
that of his surviving half-brother, but in almost every
other way a chasm lay between them. Not the least of
these was physical distance: the two never met as children.
The childhood of Yeshu, as I propose to call my father's
half-brother, is in itself a story, to be returned to later.
Here I'll merely say that he was set apart, brought up in
his mother's home town of Soochow, his very existence
hidden from my father until my grandfather was on his
deathbed and the two were already adults. As to what my
father felt on having a half-brother sprung on him, this
can only be guessed at; if his memory were a book it was
a page he left uncut, not finding it tempting to read. I
know that he went as far as acknowledging Yeshu as his
brother, but I doubt if he went any further. It was not
only that the two had grown up apart—and one loves
one's own flesh, after all, the same way as one does anybody, through adjacency and shared experience—it was

also that a shadow lay between them: the death of my father's mother, and the part that Yeshu's mother had in this. Also my father did not hold with the notion so much invoked by other Chinese: Blood is blood.

For a time the two brothers' lives were shaped by the same vicissitudes: revolution, dispossession, exile. When China went communist Yeshu moved to Hong Kong, where life as a refugee proved no less hard for him than for other Shanghainese, and days in which one prayed that something might intervene to save one—an introduction to a firm, a job, who knew?—passed with no offer of rescue. One did not realize one had so many unavailing friends until one was truly in need. The job he did finally get was not to do him much good, the company folding almost as it got going. A place was found for him in my father's business, but that, too, soon failed, and he was left once more without any means of livelihood. It was at that moment that, through his wife's family connections, the prospect presented itself of a job at a branch of the Bank of China in Canton. Another man might have said, "Anything but that, anything but going back to a country gone communist," but he at that point could only see it as a chance to extricate himself from a hopeless situation. He left for Canton in early 1951, almost believing himself the patriotic new broom the bank was encouraging him to be. His wife did not follow until three months later, delayed by an abortion forced upon her by their straitened circumstances.

There seemed, that first May Day she watched him walk past in procession with his bank colleagues, red banners arching men and women, no case for regretting their decision to return, nor for fearing any future moment in which, out of the dark, the question might rear, Is there something about him, about his fate, that dooms him to disadvantage? For, one could not be at a greater disadvantage than to be stuck in China. One could not entertain the hope, as could those who got out, that one's hour would strike, however inauspicious the start.

Years passed; then decades, an interval of complete

silence when China was cut off by an obsessive self-suffi-ciency and convulsed by the Cultural Revolution.

Now, after all those years, I was picking up the phone in the Overseas Chinese Hotel in Canton and ask-ing for Yeshu at the bank.

Expecting bureaucratic unhelpfulness, invisible men shrugging their shoulders and saying, "Never heard of him," I was surprised how easy it was to find him. I only gave his name and he was put on. After I had said who I was I could hear nothing for a few seconds. I immediately thought it was a bad connection, but it proved to be only astonished silence, for afterwards his words came out over the line to me in a rush. "Tell me where you are and I'll be over instantly."

When he appeared at the hotel I was struck by his resemblance to my grandfather. He was as slender as my father, but there the likeness ended. I had forgotten to describe myself to him, but he had no trouble picking me out from the crowd in the lobby.

I went to his home and stayed for supper—noodles eaten to flashes of Premier Zhao Ziyang on TV. After all those years one didn't think so much about the original rights and wrongs; one gave oneself to the food and met the rest of the family. His wife was animated and chatty, delighting over a small grandchild. His daughter was quiet and looked long-suffering. Years later, she told me that until I turned up in Canton, she had no idea her father had any brothers and sisters, any relatives at all, either in or outside China; she had taken him for an orphan and an only child. When my mind went back to this afterwards, it struck me to wonder if there is such a thing as an innocent secret—isn't it to lend truth power to harm, to conceal it? Can a truth, neutral to begin with, not corrupt when it is buried?

They had a two-roomed but spacious flat in a row of worn brick houses with potted plants on the balcony. A comfortable enough place, by Chinese standards. They seemed to have done well for themselves, and the thought struck me that his family background must have helped Yeshu, for it defined him as a Victim of the Decadent Old Society, the sort whose lot the past regime had set out to improve. There was a quality of life—shabby yet punctilious, hard yet reposeful, sentimental, middling, mellowed in disillusionment—that one might find in any number of socialist cities.

As we were finishing our meal the son-in-law came in, and almost the first question he asked was if the digital watch I had given Yeshu's wife was an Omega (it was a Japanese make of no particular distinction). We talked a little while longer, but we touched on nothing important. Then it was time to leave. Everyone lamented the brevity of my stay; I must come again, they said, Canton did have one or two things to offer. My hands were clasped when I said goodbye. Out of worn, silent lanes I walked into a tree-lined pond and a summer evening in a big southern port: sultry, nostalgic, long. For a communist city there were quite a few lights.

IN THE TELLING, the story of my meeting with my father's half-brother seems unremarkable, the story of any number of Chinese of my generation. Nevertheless, for me, it was a loose stitch sewn up. It was as if, finding bits missing in a file docketed "Grandmother", I had searched and turned up the mislaid pages.

That night in my hotel, I mentioned my grandmother's suicide to a colleague who had travelled to Canton with me. I said to him, "You'd think she'd come to terms with it, wouldn't you, when it was no more than what many women in her day had to put up with from their husbands?"

He said, "Maybe she was in love with him."

And I thought: That's it! How could it not have been that? I recognized the truth of what my friend suggested at first flash. I then recalled how vague Niang-niang had been, and how she had muttered something about the uncertainties of life in that age. "Perhaps it was money," she had added, unconvincingly. Nobody had thought to consider my grandmother as she was, a woman who felt herself wronged, and who wanted not to be tortured any more.

The crux of it all, it now seems plain to me, is that hers was not an arranged marriage. Arranged marriages, the bane and backbone of Chinese families, did not fall to the lot of two hard-up migrant workers; theirs was not a business of the family, not a property transaction with the partners' physical and material assets counterpoised like so many bargaining counters. So when the likes of Pearl and Jade Peach appeared, she was caught unready for the resigned acceptance that perhaps came the more easily to those who had not chosen their own husbands. Having married for love, it had never been intended that she waive her claim on her husband's fidelity.

Yet she was no better off in the end, subjected to no less humiliation than the rest of Chinese womankind. For completeness she should have had a tyrannical mother-in-law and scheming sisters-in-law, and she should have had to cope with a string of concubines.

When I think of the traditional Chinese family, I think of all the drama of the harem: the plots and the rivalries, the malice and the jealousies, the rumours, the unused energies channeling themselves into intrigues of breathtaking complexity. I have to laugh when I hear those apologists for the old Chinese family system who say that the wives and concubines lived together in perfect harmony and women had all the power, really—just think of those domineering matriarchs in fiction and history.

In fact the suggestion of discord was always there, the strain of breakdown and pain—only suppressed, one feels, by the force of habit or denial. And even the proverbial domination of the matriarch is little more than another expression of women's impotence, since it was entirely dependent on the production of sons and rarely sustained by anyone who was not prepared to devote to its attainment all her energy, skills and passion.

It was the boast of the Chinese that concubinage kept the family intact as a social unit, and was preferable to a permanent estrangement between the spouses. (Even in today's China, divorce is scarcely available as a retreat from hatred.) The question of how the women felt never came into it. No doubt many of them did not much care, one way or another; I shouldn't be at all surprised if some were simply numb—almost as if, having diverted or stifled their strongest emotions, they were left immune, feeling only the vaguest twinges of what might have been great anger or great grief. Only the few saw a solution in violent death. That is why, when my grandmother took her own life, people thought any one of half dozen reasons more probable than a broken heart.

Somerset Maugham

THE PAINTED VEIL

SHE GOT OUT of her rickshaw in the Victoria Road and walked up the steep, narrow lane till she came to the shop. She lingered outside a moment as though her attention were attracted by the bric-a-brac which was displayed. But a boy who was standing there on the watch for customers, recognizing her at once, gave her a broad smile of connivance. He said something in Chinese to someone

English novelist and short-story writer William Somerset Maugham is best known for his semi-autobiographical works, The Moon & Sixpence, Of Human Bondage, *and* The Razor's Edge. *This excerpt, from the rarely read 1924 novel* The Painted Veil, *is a classic Maugham love story, set in steamy Hong Kong.*

within and the master, a little, fat-faced man in a black gown, came out and greeted her. She walked in quickly.

"Mr. Townsend no come yet. You go top-side, yes?"

She went to the back of the shop and walked up the rickety, dark stairs. The Chinese followed her and unlocked the door that led into the bedroom. It was stuffy and there was an acrid smell of opium. She sat down on a sandal-wood chest.

In a moment she heard a heavy step on the creaking stairs. Townsend came in and shut the door behind him. His face bore a sullen look, but as he saw her it vanished, and he smiled in that charming way of his. He took her quickly in his arms and kissed her lips.

"Now what's the trouble?"

"It makes me feel better just to see you," she smiled.

He sat down on the bed and lit a cigarette.

"You look rather washed out this morning."

"I don't wonder," she answered. "I don't think I closed my eyes all night."

He gave her a look. He was smiling still, but his smile

was a little set and unnatural. She thought there was a shade of anxiety in his eyes.

"He knows," she said.

There was an instant's pause before he answered.

"What did he say?"

"He hasn't said anything."

"What!" He looked at her sharply. "What makes you think he knows then?"

"Everything. His look. The way he talked at dinner."

"Was he disagreeable?"

"No, on the contrary, he was scrupulously polite. For the first time since we married he didn't kiss me good-night."

She dropped her eyes. She was not sure if Charlie understood. As a rule Walter took her in his arms and pressed his lips to hers and would not let them go. His whole body grew tender and passionate with his kiss.

"Why do you imagine he didn't say anything?"

"I don't know."

There was a pause. Kitty sat very still on the sandal-

wood box and looked with anxious attention at
Townsend. His face once more was sullen and there was a
frown between his brows. His mouth drooped a little at
the corners. But all at once he looked up and a gleam of
malicious amusement came into his eyes.

"I wonder if he *is* going to say anything."

She did not answer. She did not know what he meant.

"After all, he wouldn't be the first man who's shut
his eyes in a case of this sort. What has he to gain by
making a row? If he'd wanted to make a row he would
have insisted on coming into your room." His eyes twin-
kled and his lips broke into a broad smile. "We should
have looked a pair of damned fools."

"I wish you could have seen his face last night."

"I expect he was upset. It was naturally a shock. It's a
damned humiliating position for any man. He always
looks a fool. Walter doesn't give me the impression of a
fellow who'd care to wash a lot of dirty linen in public."

"I don't think he would," she answered reflectively.
"He's very sensitive, I've discovered that."

"That's all to the good as far as we're concerned. You know, it's a very good plan to put yourself in some-body else's shoes and ask yourself how you would act in his place. There's only one way in which a man can save his face when he's in that sort of position and that is to pretend he knows nothing. I bet you anything you like that that is exactly what he's going to do."

The more Townsend talked the more buoyant he became. His blue eyes sparkled and he was once more his gay and jovial self. He irradiated an encouraging confidence.

"Heaven knows, I don't want to say anything dis-agreeable about him, but when you come down to brass tacks a bacteriologist is no great shakes. The chances are that I shall be Colonial Secretary when Simmons goes home, and it's to Walter's interest to keep on the right side of me. He's got his bread and butter to think of, like the rest of us: do you think the Colonial Office are going to do much for a fellow who makes a scandal? Believe me, he's got everything to gain by holding his tongue and everything to lose by kicking up a row."

Kitty moved uneasily. She knew how shy Walter was and she could believe that the fear of a scene, and the dread of public attention, might have influence upon him; but she could not believe that he would be affected by the thought of a material advantage. Perhaps she didn't know him very well, but Charlie didn't know him at all.

"Has it occurred to you that he's madly in love with me?"

He did not answer, but smiled at her with roguish eyes. She knew and loved that charming look of his.

"Well, what is it? I know you're going to say something awful."

"Well, you know, women are often under the impression that men are much more madly in love with them than they really are."

For the first time she laughed. His confidence was catching.

"What a monstrous thing to say!"

"I put it to you that you haven't been bothering much about your husband lately. Perhaps he isn't quite so much in love with you as he was."

"At all events I shall never delude myself that *you* are madly in love with me," she retorted.

"That's where you're wrong."

Ah, how good it was to hear him say that! She knew it and her belief in his passion warmed her heart. As he spoke he rose from the bed and came and sat down beside her on the sandalwood box. He put his arm round her waist.

"Don't worry your silly little head a moment longer," he said. "I promise you there's nothing to fear. I'm as certain as I am of anything that he's going to pretend he knows nothing. You know, this sort of thing is awfully difficult to prove. You say he's in love with you; perhaps he doesn't want to lose you altogether. I swear I'd accept anything rather than that if you were my wife."

She leaned towards him. Her body became limp and yielding against his arm. The love she felt for him was almost torture. His last words had struck her: perhaps Walter loved her so passionately that he was prepared to accept any humiliation if sometimes she would let him love her. She could understand that; for that was how she felt towards Charlie. A thrill of pride passed through her, and at the same time a faint sensation of contempt for a man who could love so slavishly.

She put her arm lovingly round Charlie's neck.

"You're simply wonderful. I was shaking like a leaf when I came here and you've made everything all right."

He took her face in his hand and kissed her lips.

"Darling."

"You're such a comfort to me." she sighed.

"I'm sure you need not be nervous. And you know I'll stand by you. I won't let you down."

She put away her fears, but for an instant unreasonably she regretted that her plans for the future were shattered. Now that all danger was past she almost wished that Walter were going to insist on a divorce.

"I knew I could count on you," she said.

"So I should hope."

"Oughtn't you to go and have your tiffin?"

"Oh, damn my tiffin."

He drew her more closely to him and now she was held tight in his arms. His mouth sought hers.

"Oh, Charlie, you must let me go."

"Never."

She gave a little laugh, a laugh of happy love and of triumph; his eyes were heavy with desire. He lifted her to her feet and not letting her go but holding her close to his breast he locked the door.

John Krich

THE HIGH PRICE OF
SZECHWAN CHICKEN

HONG KONG IS the bargain basement of the world. Through the barred windows of Mack's high-rise cell, we can check for shoplifters amidst Kowloon's clearance sale. Already laden with spoils in newspaper satchels, waves of Cantonese housewife commandos stage their attack. Ejected from Piccadilly double-deckers, they head straight into the department stores serpents' maws. They waddle toward sidewalk tables heaped with textile trade shards. They cram

John Krich's books have the singular ability to display simultaneously the horrors and amusements of modern travel. "The High Price of Szechwan Chicken" is from his 1984 best-seller Music in Every Room: Around the World in a Bad Mood.

into cubbyholes already stuffed with black market cassettes, Sonys instead of penny candy. They line up to pluck prizes from the glazed shooting galleries of pressed duck and fish tanks underoxygenated as the sidewalks.

Down Hanoi Road, the advertising runs horizontally, jutting at right angles from storefronts to make bridges in pictographs. Reaching around trees, the neo-neon forms trellises of words. The signs just beneath us belong to a joint that serves, "Fresh Chinese Noddles." Whatever those are, we can usually sniff them. Mack's thousand-dollar-a-month cubicle looks over an inner courtyard behind the kitchen, providing us with the panorama of a procession of cooks stealing time from their woks. Bony and fatigued in smeared aprons, they draw so hard on cigarettes that you'd think these were death row smokers. Then each haggard stir-fryer clears his chest in turn—an overture to the heaving and spitting that is Asia's congenital soundtrack. Ceaselessly, they serenade us with a song of sputum.

Is this all there is to living above a Chinese restaurant? At first browse, this town offers too many deals with too few obstacles. We want more than this watchband world that's mainly wound up, mostly practical, all price tag, part pidgin, half wholesale and two-thirds under the table. Searching, we shuttle between Kowloon and Hong Kong sides, traverse and retraverse the invisible boundaries between mislabeled First and Third Worlds. Where's the Second, and what is it, when the Third was here first? The banks and hotels built by the Brits are gray and seamless. Handsome tailored suits in concrete, not worsted. In the Chinese neighborhoods pillars that support walkway over-hangs are whitewashed, then festooned with brushstrokes in fire-engine red. This combo is old as the clash between purity and lust, spirit and blood, worker and compradores. Old as the tableaus seen in transplanted Tang Dynasty streets: a fish peddler brushing cornstarch veneer on his pile of curried octopi; a woodworker on haunches, hammering with hands that seek their task without prompting; nimbler old men kneeling at curbside to the bowl between their knees that holds customary diet of broth, noodles cushion-ing oily greens, barbecued knuckles dotted with impudent mustard; gentle goat-beards sharing a pipe and newspaper, lunchtime philosophy, visceral brotherhood; alleys stacked with warehousemen's pallets and round-hipped apothecary jars, uncut sugar cane; stores that offer only dried butter-flies, silkworm tonic and antler power; all surveyed by impassive bookkeeping girls who are mute but for the appreciation they show with a mounting ovation of abacus clicking. From these first forays, Iris and I emerge image-stuffed, dumb and wise, envious and anxious, dripping, gooey, Shanghaied, changed.

Night provides no refuge. Swaying bare bulbs turn each lane into aisles of impromptu shops, each green of British gardens into fields for competing entrepreneurial tag teams. If what they offer is duplicated a hundred times down the block, that doesn't deter these tabletop merchants. At every stall in every gutter bazaar, there's just enough action to earn tobacco, rice paper, holiday tanger-ines. Customers or no, each wheelcart chef tosses his ingredients endlessly. Here, every man is his own supply and demand. Underdevelopment, as we should have known, as we still have to learn, is really an overdevelopment of need: too many trying to sell to too many who cannot buy.

Yet few seem so poor that they can't pick out their own live carp for supper or pick a winning horse at the races. Iris and I find that out when we're trapped in a riot for the few remaining grandstand seats at the track that's misnamed Happy Valley. Not only do few of the bettors look happy, but the hills on all sides are covered in the Chinese cemeteries' crazy cross-hatching. The tombstones aren't neat, Presbyterian rows, but tilted to join nature's chaos and catch the proper fêng shui, we know. Before the afterlife, before the last exacta, there's time to gamble on "Empress Wan," to make one last stab at good fortune—which, the Chinese wisely admit, will take a man farther than talent. Where's that geomancer to give us a tip when we need it? Our gray mare finishes out of the running. "Sometimes lucky, sometimes no luck," murmur the denizens of Happy Valley. And Hong Kong itself is but a long shot, lease expiring. It's one big bookie joint operating under the nose of the Maoist vice squad. It's a gamble against the future but the lines at the wager windows keep getting longer.

Where do the winnings go? Some get dragged up the peaks to estates whose walls are capped by broken glass; some get invested in Rolls-Royces that come by the bushel; some pay to erect a statue of one's diminutive self, as in the case of Doctor Aw, inventor of Tiger Balm—that Asian Ben-Gay, which makes the Asiatic claim to sooth all manner of soreness, even spiritual—who's immortalized himself in business suit, overlooking the porcelain phantasmagoria of his Tiger Balm Gardens. Lesser bankrolls buy gadgets that get smuggled out to appliance-hungry relatives in the mother country. One day's pari-mutuel provides helpings of Szechwan chicken devoured in galleys of sampans moored in the dark. Here, pleasures are not so much savored as hoarded.

In this materialist enclave, there's little argument about what people want, and only infrequently about how to get it. The Brits run a high volume, low overhead trading post; they offer one prized rock's worth of real estate on which cling the addicts of property. Hong Kong, divided into two cultures, remains a solid-state colony. Shake it like a digital nine-band dream-bar clock radio you want to buy—and let the buyer beware! Tickle those transistors. Turn this model upside-down. The circuitry won't come loose. There's no rattle.

Where everything comes duty-free, nothing comes free of duty. Six days and sixty hours are the average work week, a perennial version of the Christmas overtime that's got Iris and me here. Only these workers aren't planning any jaunts. With the tacit approval of their Communist confreres, they remain prisoners of the "balance of payments," unprotected, democracy's coolies. Inside Kowloon's fabric factories, nearly naked men breathe cotton candy air, place bare feet close to the cutting edge of the presses. Their comrades must fit the huge bales into truck trailers—a Chinese puzzle solved by overexertion. Their sisters sew Parisian names and price tags into blue jeans, trapped in a sunless, surfless riviera of sweatshops.

Though barely in Asia, we're acquiring a heightened sense of all cities as stationary fronts in a war. Factotum against peon, colonialist versus tong, banking cartel aimed at politburo: a tussle goes on for souls by the millions and paper money by the trillions. But each side seems so enlivened by their maneuvering that none are eager to impose the stillness of outright victory, all aim for mere upping of stalemate. The result, if there's any, is to be found in the gradual, gnawing "betterment of man," usually measured by square feet of housing per occupant, nearly unrecognizable when it arrives, certainly unknown by those who are its martyrs. Even the beggars of Hong Kong, those human filings drawn to the sidewalk magnet, lying face down in strategic placement, seem to be answering a distant command by offering themselves for trampling. These are foot soldiers who have fallen in place. "Sometimes lucky, sometimes no luck." They, too, are members in good standing of an army on yet another long march.

Louise Ho

CITY

NO FINGERS CLAW at the bronze gauze
Of a Hong Kong December dusk,
Only a maze of criss-crossing feet
That enmeshes the city
In a merciless grid.

Native Hong Kong-er Louise Ho is a lecturer at the Chinese University Hong Kong, where she teaches Shakespeare and eighteenth-century poetry. "City" is her contribution to a new collection of young, hip Chinese poetry called vs. 12: Hong Kong Poems.

Between many lanes
Of traffic, the street-sleeper
Carves out his island home.
Or under the thundering fly-over,
Another makes his peace of mind.

Under the staircase,
By the public lavatory,
A man entirely unto himself
Lifts his hand
And opens his palm.
His digits
Do not rend the air,
They merely touch
As pain does, effortlessly.

Ian Fleming

HONG KONG

IF YOU WRITE thrillers, people think that you must live a thrilling life and enjoy doing thrilling things. Starting with these false assumptions, the Editorial Board of the *Sunday Times* repeatedly urged me to do something exciting and write about it, and at the end of October 1959 they came up with the idea that I should make a round trip of the most exciting cities of the world and describe them in beautiful, beautiful prose.

English novelist Ian Fleming (1908–1964) is best known for his spy thrillers featuring the dashing James Bond. A 1964 travel book, Thrilling Cities, *profiled several of Fleming's favorite destinations, among them Hong Kong.*

This could be accomplished, they said, within a month.

Dubiously, I discussed this project with Mr. Leonard Russell, features and literary editor of the paper. I said it was going to be very expensive and very exhausting, and that one couldn't go round the world in thirty days and report either beautifully or accurately on great cities in approximately three days per city. I also said that I was the world's worst sight-seer and that I had often advocated the provision of roller-skates at the doors of museums and art galleries. I was also, I said, impatient of lunching at Government Houses and of visiting clinics and resettlement areas.

Leonard Russell was adamant. "We don't want that sort of thing," he said. "In your James Bond books, even if people can't put up with James Bond and those fancy heroines of yours, they seem to like the exotic backgrounds. Surely you want to pick up some more material for your stories? This is a wonderful opportunity."

I objected that my stories were fiction and the sort

of things that happened to James Bond didn't happen in real life.

"Rot," he said firmly.

So, wishing privately to see the world, however rapidly, while it was still there to see, I purchased a round-the-world air ticket for £803 19s. 2d., drew £500 in travellers' cheques from the chief accountant, and had several "shots" which made me feel sore and rather dizzy. Then, on November 2nd, armed with a sheaf of visas, a round-the-world suit with concealed money pockets, one suit-case in which, as one always does, I packed more than I needed, and my typewriter, I left humdrum London for the thrilling cities of the world—Hong Kong, Macao, Tokyo, Honolulu, Los Angeles, Las Vegas, Chicago, New York.

On that soft, grey morning, Comet G/ADOK shot up so abruptly from the north-south runway of London Airport that the beige curtains concealing the lavatories and the cockpit swayed back to the cabin at an angle of

fifteen degrees. The first soaring leap through the over-
cast was to ten thousand feet. There was a slight tremor
as we went through the lower cloud base and another as
we came out into the brilliant sunshine.

We climbed on another twenty thousand feet into
that world above the cotton-wool cloud carpet where it is
always a beautiful day. The mind adjusted itself to the
prospect of twenty-four hours of this sort of thing—the
hot face and rather chilly feet, eyes that smart with the
outside brilliance, the smell of Elizabeth Arden and
Yardley cosmetics that B.O.A.C. provide for their passengers, the varying whine of the jets, the first cigarette of
an endless chain of smoke, and the first conversational
gambits exchanged with the seatfellow who, in this
instance, was a pleasant New Zealander with a flow of
aboriginal jokes and nothing else to do but talk the
whole way to Hong Kong.

Zürich came and the banal beauty of Switzerland,
then the jagged sugar-icing of the Alps, the blue pud-

dles of the Italian lakes and the snow melting down towards the baked terrazzo of the Italian plains. My companion commented that we had a good seat "view-wise," not like the other day when he was crossing the Atlantic and an American woman came aboard and complained when she found herself sitting over the wing. "It's always the same," she had cried. "When I get on an aircraft, all I can see outside is wing." The American next to her had said, "Listen, ma'am, you go right on seeing that wing. Start worrying when you can't see it any longer."

Below us Venice was an irregular brown biscuit surrounded by the crumbs of her islands. A straggling crack in the biscuit was the Grand Canal. At six hundred miles an hour, the Adriatic and the distant jagged line of Yugoslavia were gone in half an hour. Greece was blanketed in cloud, and we were out over the eastern Mediterranean in the time it took to consume a cupful of B.O.A.C. fruit salad. (My neighbor told me he liked sweet things. When I got to Los Angeles, I must be sure and not forget to eat poison-berry pie.)

It was now two o'clock in the afternoon, G.M.T., but we were travelling towards the night and dusk came to meet us. An hour more of slow, spectacular sunset and blue-black night and then Beirut showed up ahead—a sprawl of twinkling hundreds-and-thousands under an *Arabian Nights* new moon that dived down into the oil lands as the Comet banked to make her landing. Beirut is a crooked town, and when we came to rest, I advised my neighbour to leave nothing small on his seat, and particularly not his extremely expensive camera. I said that we were now entering the thieving areas of the world. Someone would get it. The hatch clanged open, and the first sticky fingers of the East reached in.

"Our Man in Lebanon" was there to meet me, full of the gossip of the bazaars. Beirut is the great smuggling junction of the world. Diamonds thieved from Sierra Leone come in here for onward passage to Germany, cigarettes and pornography from Tangier, arms for the sheikhs of Araby and drugs from Turkey. Gold? Yes, said my friend. Did I remember the case brought by the Bank of England in the Italian courts against a ring that was minting real gold sovereigns containing the exactly correct amount of gold? The Bank of England had finally won their case in Switzerland, but now another ring had gone one better. They were minting gold sovereigns in Aleppo and now saving a bit on the gold content. These were for India. Only last week there had been a big Indian buyer in Beirut. He had bought sacks of sovereigns and flown them to a neighbouring port, where he had put them on board his private yacht. Then he sailed to Goa in Portuguese India. From there, with the help of conniving Indian frontier officials, the gold would go on its way to the bullion brokers in Bombay. There was still this mad thirst for gold in India. The premium was not what it had been after the war, only about sixty per cent now instead of the old three hundred per cent, but it was still well worth the trouble and occasional danger.

Opium? Yes, there was a steady stream coming in from Turkey; also heroin, which is refined opium, from Germany via Turkey and Syria. Every now and then the American Federal Narcotics Bureau in Rome would trace a gang back to Beirut and, with the help of local police, there would be a raid and a handful of prison sentences. But Interpol, our man urged, should have an office in Beirut. There would be plenty to keep them busy. I asked where all the drugs were going to. To Rome and then down to Naples for shipment to America. That's where the consumption was, and the big prices. Arms smuggling wasn't doing too well now that Cyprus was more or less settled. Beirut had been the centre of that traffic—mostly Italian and Belgian arms—but now there was only a trickle going over, and the sheikhs had enough of the light stuff and wanted tanks and planes, and these were too big to smuggle.

We sat sipping thin lemonade in the pretentious, empty airport with scabby walls and sand blown from the desert on the vast, empty floors. The doors had been locked upon us and our passports impounded by surly Lebanese police. Flight announcements were first in Arabic—the hall-mark of a small state playing at power. It was good to get back to one's comfortable seat in the Comet and to be offered chewing-gum by a beautiful Indian stewardess in an emerald sari with gold trim—not only the "magic carpet" routine but necessary to cope with our changing groups of local passengers. We soared up again into the brilliant night sky, and then there was nothing but the desert and, forty thousand feet below, the oil wells flaring in the night. (My neighbour said that the lavatories at Beirut had been dreadful. He added that in an Iowa hotel the lavatories were marked "Pointers" and "Setters.")

I had armed myself for the flight with the perfect book for any journey—Eric Ambler's wonderful thriller *Passage of Arms*, a proof copy of which had been given to me by Mr. Frere of Heinemann's for the trip. I had only been able to read a few pages and I was now determined

to get back to it. I offered another book to my neighbour, but he said he hadn't got much time for books. He
said that whenever someone asked him whether he had
read this or that, he would say, "No, sir. But have you
red hairs on your chest?" I said that I was sorry but I
simply must read my book as I had to review it. The lie
was effective, and my companion went off to sleep, hog-
ging more than his share of the arm-rest.

Bahrein is, without question, the scruffiest international airport in the world. The washing facilities would
not be tolerated in a prison, and the slow fans in the
ceilings of the bedraggled hutments hardly stirred the
flies. Stale, hot air blew down off the desert, and there
was a chirrup of unknown insects. A few onlookers shuffled about with their feet barely off the ground, spitting
and scratching themselves. This is the East one is glad to
get through quickly.

Up again over the Arabian Sea with, below us, the
occasional winking flares of the smuggling dhows that hug

the coast from India down past the Aden Protectorate and East Africa, carrying cargoes of illegal Indian emigrants on their way to join fathers and uncles and cousins in the cheap labour markets of Kenya and Tanganyika. Without passports, they are landed on the African continent anywhere south of the equator and disappear into the bidonvilles that are so much more hospitable than the stews of Bombay. From now on we shall be in the lands of baksheesh, squeeze, and graft, which rule from the smallest coolie to the Mr. Bigs in government.

Ten thousand feet below us a baby thunderstorm flashed violent. My neighbour said he must get a picture of it, groped under his seat. Consternation! A hundred and fifty pounds' worth of camera and lenses had been filched! Already the loot would be on its way up the pipe-line to the bazaars. The long argument with the chief steward about responsibility and insurance went on far across the great black vacuum of India.

More thunderstorms fluttered in the foothills of the

Himalayas while B.O.A.C. stuffed us once again, like
Strasbourg geese, with food and drink. I had no idea what
time it was or when I was going to get any sleep between
these four or five-hour leaps across the world. My watch
said midnight G.M.T., and this tricked me into drinking a
whisky-and-soda in the pretentious airport at New Delhi,
where the sad Benares brassware in unsaleable Indian
shapes and sizes collects dust in the forlorn show-cases.
Alas, before I had finished it, a pale dawn was coming up
and great flocks of awakened crows fled silently overhead
towards some distant breakfast among the rubbish dumps
outside India's capital.

India has always depressed me. I can't bear the universal dirt and squalor and the impression, false I am
sure, that everyone is doing no work except living off
his neighbour. And I am desolated by the *outward* manifestations of the two great Indian religions. Ignorant,
narrow-minded, bigoted? Of course I am. But perhaps
this extract from India's leading newspaper, boxed and in

heavy black type on the back page of the *Statesman* of November 21st, 1959, will help to excuse my prejudices:

10 YEARS' PRISON FOR KIDNAPPING

New Delhi, Nov. 16. A bill providing deterrent punishment for kidnapping minors and maiming and employing them for begging, was introduced in the Lok Sabha today by the Home Minister, Pandit Pant.

The bill seeks to amend the relevant sections of the Indian Penal Code, and provides for imprisonment extending up to 10 years and fine in the case of kidnapping or obtaining custody of minors for employing them for begging, and life imprisonment and fine in the case of maiming.

BACK ON THE plane, the assistant stewardess wore the Siamese equivalent of a cheongsam. Five hours away was Bangkok. One rejected sleep and breakfast for the splendour below and away to port, where the Himalayas shone proudly and the tooth of Everest looked small and easy to climb. Why had no one ever told me that the mouths of the Ganges are one of the wonders of the world? Gigantic brown meanderings between walls and islands of olive green, each one of a hundred tributaries seeming ten times the size of the Thames. A short neck of the Bay of Bengal and then down over the rice-fields of Burma to the heavenly green pastures of Thailand, spread out among wandering rivers and arrow-straight canals like some enchanted garden. This was the first place of really startling beauty I had so far seen, and the temperature of ninety-two degrees in the shade on the tarmac did nothing to spoil the impact of the country where I would advise other travellers to have their first view of the true Orient. The minute air hostess, smiling the first true smile, as opposed to an air-hostess smile, since London, told us to "forrow me."

In spite of the mosquitoes as large as Messerschmitts and the wringing humidity, everyone seems to agree that

Bangkok is a dream city, and I blamed myself for hurrying on to Hong Kong. In only one hour one still got the impression of the topsy-turvy, childlike quality of the country, and an old Siamese hand, a chance acquaintance, summed it up with a recent cutting from a Bangkok newspaper. This was a plaintive article by a high police official remonstrating with tourists for accosting girls in the streets. These street-walkers were unworthy representatives of Siamese womanhood. A tourist had only to call at the nearest police station to be given names and addresses and prices of not only the most beautiful, but the most respectable, girls in the city!

Back in the Comet that, after six thousand miles, seemed as fresh and trim as it had at London Airport, it was half an hour across the China Sea before one's clothes came unstuck from one's body. Then it was only another hour or so before the Chinese Communist-owned outer islands of Hong Kong showed up below and we began to drift down to that last little strip of tarmac set in one of the most beautiful views in the world. It was nearly five o'clock and just over twenty-six hours and seven thousand miles from London. Twenty minutes late! Take a letter please, Miss Trueblood.

"Is MORE BETTER now, Master?"

I grunted luxuriously, and the velvet hands withdrew from my shoulders. More Tiger Balm was applied to the fingertips, and then the hands were back, now to massage the base of my neck with soft authority. Through the open French windows the song of bulbuls came from the big orchid tree covered with deep pink blossom, and two Chinese magpies chattered in the grove of casuarina. Somewhere far away turtle-doves were saying "coocoroo." Number-one boy (number one from among seven in the house) came in to say that breakfast was ready on the veranda. I exchanged compliments with the dimpling masseuse, put on a shirt and trousers and sandals, and walked out into the spectacular, sundrenched view.

As, half-way through the delicious scrambled eggs and bacon, a confiding butterfly, black and cream and dark blue, settled on my wrist, I reflected that heaven could wait. Here, on the green and scarcely inhabited slopes of Shek-O, above Big Wave Bay on the south-east corner of Hong Kong island, was good enough.

This was my first morning in Hong Kong, and this small paradise was the house of friends, Mr. and Mrs. Hugh Barton. Hugh Barton is perhaps the most powerful surviving English *taipan* (big shot) in the Orient, and he lives in discreet accordance with his status as Chairman of Messrs. Jardine Matheson, the great Far Eastern trading corporation founded by energetic Scotsmen one hundred and forty years ago. They say in Hong Hong that power resides in the Jockey Club, Jardine Matheson, the Hong Kong and Shanghai Bank, and Her Majesty's Government —in that order. Hugh Barton, being a steward of the Jockey Club, Chairman of Jardines, Deputy Chairman of the Hong Kong and Shanghai Bank, and a member of the Governor's Legislative Council, has it every way, and when I complained of a mildly stiff neck after my flight, it was natural that so powerful a *taipan's* household should conjure up a comely masseuse before breakfast. That is the right way, but alas how rare, for powerful *taipan's* to operate. When, the night before, I had complimented Mrs. Barton for having fixed a supremely theatrical new moon for my arrival, I was not being all that fanciful.

Apart from being the last stronghold of feudal luxury in the world, Hong Kong is the most vivid and exciting city I have ever seen, and I recommend it without reserve to anyone who possesses the fare. It seems to have every-thing—modern comfort in a theatrically Oriental setting; and equable climate except during the monsoons; beautiful country for walking or riding; all sports, including the finest golf course—the Royal Hong Kong—in the East, the most expensively equipped race-course, and wonderful skin-diving; exciting flora and fauna, including the celebrated butterflies of Hong Kong; and a cost of living that compares favourably with any other tourist city. Minor attractions include really good Western and Chinese restaurants, exotic night-life, cigarettes at IS. 3d. for twenty, and heavy Shantung silk suits, shirts, etc., expertly tailored in forty-eight hours.

With these and innumerable other advantages it is, therefore, not surprising that the population of this minute territory is over three million, or one million more than the whole of New Zealand. The fact that six hundred and fifty million Communist Chinese are a few miles away across the frontier seems only to add zest to the excitement at all levels of life in the colony, and from the Governor down, if there is an underlying tension, there is certainly no dismay. Obviously China could take Hong Kong by a snap of its giant fingers, but China has shown no signs of wishing to do so, and when the remaining forty years of our lease of the mainland territory expire, I see no reason why a reduced population should not retreat to the islands and the original territory, which Britain holds in perpetuity.

Whatever the future holds, there is no sign that a sinister, doom-fraught count-down is in progress. It is true that the colony every now and then gets the shivers, but when an American bank pulled up stumps during the Quemoy troubles in 1958, there was nothing but mockery. The government pressed on inside the leased territory with the building of the largest hospital in the Orient and with the erection of an average of two schools a month to meet the influx of refugees from China. The private Chinese and European builders also pressed on, and continue to press on today, with the construction of twenty-story apartment houses for the lower and middle classes. Altogether it is a gay and splendid colony humming with vitality and progress, and pure joy to the senses and spirits.

Apart from my host, my guide, philosopher, and friend in Hong Kong, and later in Japan, was "Our Man in the Orient," Richard Hughes, Far Eastern correspondent of the *Sunday Times*. He is a giant Australian with a European mind and a quixotic view of the world exemplified by his founding of the Baritsu branch of the Baker Street Irregulars—Baritsu is Japanese for the national code of self-defence which includes judo, and is the only Japanese word known to have been used by Sherlock Holmes.

On my first evening he and I went out on the town.

The streets of Hong Kong are the most enchanting night streets I have ever trod. Here the advertising agencies are ignorant of the drab fact, known all too well in London and New York, that patterns of black and red and yellow have the most compelling impact on the human eye. Avoiding harsh primary colours, the streets of Hong Kong are evidence that neon lighting need not be hideous, and the crowded Chinese ideograms in pale violet and pink and green with a plentiful use of white are entrancing not only for their colours but also because on does not know what drab messages and exhortations they spell out. The smell of the streets is sea-clean with an occasional exciting dash of sandalwood from a joss-stick factory, frying onions, and the scent of sweet perspiration that underlies Chinese cooking. The girls, thanks to the cheongsams they wear, have a deft and coltish prettiness which sends Western women into paroxysms of envy. The high, rather stiff collar of the cheongsam gives authority and poise to the head and shoulders, and the flirtatious slits from the hem of the dress upwards, as high as the beauty of the leg will allow, demonstrate that the sex appeal of the inside of a woman's knee has apparently never occurred to Dior or Balmain. No doubt there are fat or dumpy Chinese women in Hong Kong, but I never saw one. Even the men, in their spotless white shirts and dark trousers, seem to have better, fitter figures than we in the West, and the children are a constant enchantment.

We started off our evening at the solidest bar in Hong Kong—the sort of place that Hemingway liked to write about, lined with ships' badges and other trophies, with, over the bar, a stuffed alligator with an iguana riding on its back. The bar belongs to Jack Conder, a former Shanghai municipal policeman and reputed to have been the best pistol shot there in the old days. His huge fists seem to hold the memory of many a recalcitrant chin. He will not allow women in the bar downstairs on the grounds that real men should be allowed to drink alone. When the Japanese came in 1941, Conder stayed on in Shanghai, was captured, and escaped. He took the long walk all the way down China to Chungking, sleeping during daylight hours in graveyards, where the ghosts effectively protected him. He is the authentic Hemingway type and he sells solid drinks at reasonable prices. His bar is the meeting-place of "Alcoholics Synonymous"—a group of lesser Hemingway characters, most of them local press correspondents. The initiation ceremony requires the consumption of sixteen San Migs, which is the pro name for the local San Miguel beer—to my taste a very unencouraging brew.

After fortification with Western poisons (I gather that no self-respecting Chinese would think of drinking before dinner, but that the fashion for whisky is invading the Orient almost as fast as it has invaded France) we proceeded to one of the finest Chinese locales, the Peking Restaurant. Dick Hughes, a hard-bitten Orientalogue, was determined that I should become Easternized as soon as possible and he missed no opportunity to achieve the conversion. The Peking Restaurant was bright and clean. We consumed seriatim:

> shark's fin soup with crab,
> shrimp balls in oil,
> bamboo shoots with seaweed,
> chicken and walnuts,

with, as a main dish,

> roast Peking duckling,

washed down with mulled wine. Lotus seeds in syrup added a final gracious touch.

Dick insisted that then, and on all future occasions when we were together, I should eat with chopsticks, and I pecked around with these graceful but ridiculous instruments with clumsy enthusiasm. To my surprise the meal, most elegantly presented and served, was in every respect delicious. All the tastes were new and elusive, but I was particularly struck with another aspect of Oriental cuisine— each dish had a quality of gaiety about it, assisted by discreet ornamentation, so that the basically unattractive process of shovelling food into one's mouth achieved, whether one liked it or not, a kind of elegance. And the background to this, and to all my subsequent meals in the East, always had this quality of gaiety—people chattering happily and smiling with pleasure and encouragement. From now on all the meals I ate in authentic, as opposed to tourist, Chinese or Japanese restaurants were infinitely removed from what, for a lifetime, and been a dull, rather unattractive routine in the sombre eating mills of the West, where the customer, his neighbours, and the waiters seem subtly to resent each other, the fact that they should all be there together, and very often the things they are eating.

Dick Hughes spiced our banquet with the underground and underworld gossip of the colony—the inability of the government to deal drastically with Hong Kong's only real problem, the water shortage. Why didn't they hand it over to private enterprise? The gas and electricity services were splendidly run by the Kadoorie brothers, whose record had been equally honourable in Shanghai. There was a grave shortage of hotels. Why didn't Jardines do something about it? Japanese mistresses were preferable to Chinese girls. If, for one reason or another, you fell out with your Japanese girl, she would be dignified, philosophical. But the Chinese girl would throw endless hysterical scenes and probably turn up at your office and complain to your employer. Servants? They were plentiful and wonderful, but too many of the English and American wives had no idea how to treat food servants. They would clap their hands and shout "Boy!" to cover their lack of self-confidence. This sort of behaviour was out of fashion and brought the Westerner into disrepute. (How often one has heard the same thing said of English wives in other "coloured" countries!)

The latest public scandal was the massage parlours and the blue cinemas (with colour and sound!) that flourished, particularly across the harbour in Kowloon. The *Hong Kong Standard* had been trying to clean them up. The details they had published had anyway been good for circulation. He read out from the *Standard*: "Erotic dailies circulate freely here. Blue films shown openly. Hong Kong police round up massage girls." The *Standard* had given the names and addresses: "Miss Ten Thousand Fun and Safety at 23 Stanley Street, 2nd floor. Business starting at 9 A.M. . . . Miss Soft and Warm Village. . . . Miss Outer Space and Miss Lotus of Love at 17 Café Apartments, Room 113, ground floor. (Opposite the French Hospital. Room heated). . . . Miss Chaste and Refined, Flat A, Percival Mansion, 6th floor (life service)." And more wonderful names: "Miss Smooth and Fragrant. . . Miss Emerald Parsley. . . Miss Peach Stream Pool (satisfaction guaranteed)," and so forth.

The trouble, explained Dick, was partly the traditional desire of Oriental womanhood to please, combined with unemployment and the rising cost of living. Increase in the number of light industries, particularly the textile mills, the bane of Lancashire and America, might help. Would I like to visit the latest textile mill? I said I wouldn't.

It was a natural step from this conversation to proceed from the Peking Restaurant to the world of Suzie Wong.

Richard Mason, with his splendid book *The World of Suzie Wong*, has done for a modest water-front hotel what Hemingway did for his very different Harry's Bar in Venice. The book, though, like *A Many-Splendoured Thing* by Han Suyin, read universally by the literate in Hong Kong, is small-mindedly frowned upon, largely I gather because miscegenation with beautiful Chinese girls in understandably an unpopular topic with the great union of British woman-hood. But the Suzie Wong myth is in Hong Kong to stay, and Richard Mason would be amused to find how it has gathered depth and detail.

It seems to be fact, for instance, and perhaps the only known fact, that when he was in Hong Kong Richard Mason did live in a water-front establishment called the Luk Kwok Hotel, transformed in his book into the Nam Kok House of Pleasure, where the painter, Robert Lomax, befriended and, after comic, tender, romantic, and finally tragic interludes, married the charming prostitute Suzie Wong.

As a result of the book, the Luk Kwok Hotel, so conveniently placed near the fleet landing-stage and the British Sailors' Home, has boomed. Solitary girls still may not sit unaccompanied in the spacious bar with its great and manysplendoured juke box. You must still bring them in from outside, as did Lomax, to prevent the hotel becoming, legally, a disorderly house. But the whole place has been redecorated in deep battleship grey (to remind the sailors of home?), and one of Messrs. Collin's posters advertising Richard Mason's book has a place of honour on the main wall. Other signs of prosperity are a huge and hideous near-Braque on another wall, a smart Anglepoise light over the cash register, and a large bowl of Siamese fighting fish. (It is also a sign of fame, of which the proprietor is very proud, that the totally respectable Prime Minister of Laos and his Foreign Minister stayed at the Luk Kwok on a visit to Hong Kong.)

If you enquire after Suzie herself, you are answered with a melancholy shake of the head and the sad, dramatic news that Suzie's marriage failed and she is now back "on the pipe." When you ask where you could find her, it is explained that she will see no other man and waits for Lomax one day to return. She is not in too bad a way, as Lomax sends her regular remittances from London. But there are many other beautiful girls here just as beautiful as

Suzie. Would you care to meet one, a very particular friend of Suzie's?

I don't know how much the sailors believe this story, but I suspect they are all quite happy to put up with "Suzie's friend," and I for one greatly enjoyed exploring the myth that will for ever inhabit the Luk Kwok Hotel with its neon slogans: "GIRLS, BUT NO OBLIGATION TO BUY DRINKS! CLEAN SURROUNDINGS! ENJOY TO THE MAX-IMUM AT THE LEAST EXPENSE!"

Dick Hughes misunderstood one author's delighted interest in the brilliance of another author's myth and protested that there were far better establishments awaiting my patronage. But by now it was late and the after-effects of jet travel—a dull headache and a bronchial breathless-ness—had caught up with me, and we ended our evening with a walk along the thronged quays in search of a taxi and home.

On the way I commented on the fact that there is not a single sea-gull in the whole vast expanse of Hong Kong harbour. Dick waved towards the dense flood of junks and sampans on which families of up to half a dozen spend the whole of their lives, mostly tied up in harbour. There hadn't used to be any sea-gulls in Shanghai either, he said. Since the communists took over they have come back. The communists have put it about that they had come back because they no longer have to fight with the humans for the harbour refuse. It was probably the same thing in Hong Kong. It would take an awful lot of sea-gulls to compete for a living with three million Chinese.

On this downbeat note I closed my first enchanted day.

Susannah Hoe

POOR MARY ANN AND THE ROBBERS

THE INDIGENOUS INHABITANTS of Hong Kong Island before and after 1841 were, on the whole, peaceful, and not hostile towards the Westerners who came to settle. Those Chinese who started immediately to arrive from the mainland were of a different mind; like many of the Westerners, they were there for the pickings. Robbery and piracy were rife.

Novelist and biographer Susannah Hoe's most recent book is a collection of tales called The Private Life of Old Hong Kong *(1991). The stories detail the wild and woolly experiences of western women in nineteenth-century Hong Kong, including Poor Mary Ann.*

Brigandage was not the only problem. The August 1842 Treaty of Nanking was meant to end the First Opium War; Hong Kong was in British hands and five mainland ports, including Canton, were opened up to foreign trade. In Canton, trading was no longer to be only through designated Chinese merchants, and families were allowed to live in the foreign factories. In practice it was not quite so easy.

In the 1840s the watery triangle of Canton, Hong Kong and Macau was to become a well-travelled trail. If there was too much heat, too much illness, or too much trouble in one place, residents, particularly women and children, would move for a few weeks. Friendship between women then was important, as mothers with a brood of children in tow would descend on each other to escape their usual environment.

One of the factors forcing women temporarily out of Canton was that the ordinary Chinese there took time to accept them. What happened in December 1842 was the most violent manifestation of a series of upsets. The riots were a natural result of a treaty under which the Chinese had finally to accept defeat; it created fertile soil for rumour and increased fear and hatred of the barbarian.

It is said that the riots were caused by the thoughtless appearance in Canton of "three or four English ladies (wives of captains of the ships at Whampoa) in the streets of Canton". It was not just that they were foreign women, according to W. D. Bernard of the *Nemesis,* but that the sight of women was so against custom: Chinese "ladies" were never seen in public except in secluded sedan chairs. A few days after that first expedition, the same women came to live in one of the factories, which was then the first to be attacked during the riots.

Who were those women? It is no doubt out of delicacy that Bernard fails to name them but the lack of a name under such circumstances always arouses suspicion. After the riots, a group of foreign merchants in Canton wrote to Sir Henry Pottinger, the British Plenipotentiary, about them.

They talked of the wives being those of "accidental visitors", not resident merchants. Again, no names.

One named woman was in Canton during that period and was involved in those riots, but she was not British, and she was not a merchant's wife or a captain's wife. She was Harriet Parker, wife of the American medical missionary Dr. Peter Parker. He had been practising in Canton for some years and had only recently brought back from America with him the former Miss Webster—young, "very pretty and amiable", and pious.

Peter Parker at first left Harriet in Macau but having reestablished himself in his hospital in Canton, he took her there on 5 November 1842. She is known as the first Western woman to live, rather than stay temporarily, in China, and she took great pains to be discreet. Parker wrote about that first day: "It was not perceived that a foreign lady was in the boat as we came up the river, and, wishing to avoid a tumult immediately on landing, we walked to the American factory. As we passed through the company's factory the crowd began to collect to see the foreign lady."

A linguist was sent by the Chinese authorities to ascertain the Parkers' intentions and was reassured; although Mrs. Parker was there permanently, she did not want to cause trouble and would not venture into the streets. But from the terrace where she walked in the evening she could be seen from the tops of the houses.

On 23 December, Parker wrote to his sister about what had happened:

Alas! in an evil hour our peace and quietness were disturbed from our proximity to the English, who, in the course of the late war, had rendered themselves particularly obnoxious to the Chinese. On the eighth instant, a quarrel with a lascar [Indian sailor] became the occasion for the pent-up feeling to manifest itself in the burning of the English factory and the plunder of nearly half a million dollars in specie [coins].

The scene was one that defies description. Hatty, with her friend, Mrs. Isaacson, an English lady who was making her a visit, were moved early to Mingkwa's factory, the Chinese factory next to the American . . . and the next morning without any difficulty was removed to Whampoa, where she has since been kindly and hospitably entertained on board the *Splendid* and the *Oneida.* In one or two days more I think of her returning with me to Canton, as all is quiet now, and I have so many friends among the Chinese, as well as foreigners, that, on the approach of a similar riot, it would be easy for her to escape; besides there is no present prospect of such an occurrence again.

IN BERNARD'S VERSION, he reports that the anonymous English merchants' wives "escaped, with the utmost difficulty and danger, by a back way, and were received in one of the Hong merchants warehouses until they could be conveyed down the river. But the mob destroyed and tore into shreds every article of their wardrobe which they could find."

Harriet Parker returned to Canton on the evening of Christmas day, and stayed, though there are constant sightings of her visiting Macau and Hong Kong in the years that followed. Eighteen months later, a *Friend of China* editorial declared:

There is a continued manifestation of the ill feeling entertained towards foreigners by the Chinese, which have resulted in one or two riots which although not of a very serious nature, tend, with other circumstances, to make Canton a disagreeable and dangerous place of residence. Numbers of idle vagabonds keep prowling round the factories, bent upon mischief; and the sight of a lady walking in the Company's garden is quite enough to cause an excitement, the mob getting upon the walls and staring in the most annoying manner.

The next time the newspaper discussed the issue, it was used as an occasion to belabour Admiral Cochrane, the naval commander; he seemed to care little that "many of his fair countrywomen are exposed to the brutality of degraded beings, whom we are ashamed to be compelled to look upon as fellow men."

IT WAS SIX months after Harriet Parker's escape that Elizabeth Brown experienced similar unpleasantness in Hong Kong, and barely a year after that it was Mary Ann Le Foy's turn. In both those last two cases, however, the motive appeared to be robbery, rather than a manifestation of hatred; destruction, though, was once again a feature.

The *Friend of China* wrote of the first incident on 9 May 1843:

An attack was made by Robbers upon the house of the Morrisonian Education Society; Mr. Brown was stabbed in two places. The robbers drove all the inmates from the house, of which they had full possession for two hours and only decamped at daylight. Dr. Hobson, Mr. Brown, and Mr. Morrison lost some property, and HE the Plenipotentiary's great seal was stolen.

WHAT THAT REPORT omits to say is that the Reverend Samuel Brown had a wife, and that she was with him. In his detailed account of the incident, Brown's biographer mentions only Samuel and Elizabeth Brown, their two children, Julia aged four, Robert, a babe in arms, Dr. McCartee, a visiting missionary, and some Chinese boys—pupils who lived in.

Elizabeth Brown was not a nonentity whose presence might have been missed by any but a careless reporter. The American educationalist and missionary, Samuel Robbins Brown, married Elizabeth Bartlet, daughter of a Connecticut clergyman, on 10 October 1838 and sailed with her for China a week later. They arrived in Macau in February 1839. The most appealing account of Elizabeth is by William Low, Harriet Low's brother, who arrived in China as a clerk after she had left. He went to tea with Elizabeth in August 1839 and wrote:

> It did me good to see some white ladies I assure you. Mrs. Brown is a very good looking woman indeed, and quite young. I hauled alongside of her as quick as possible, and had quite a confab. She looked good enough to eat, I did not talk as long with her, as I should like to have done, as I wanted to give others a chance, and then I did not want her hubby to get jealous—hem . . .

BROWN HAD BEEN recruited to run the Morrison Education Society's school in Macau and he opened it soon after his arrival in the house that Mary Gutzlaff had used for her school before the August 1839 evacuation.

The school was removed from Macau to Hong Kong in November 1842, to what is today called Morrison Hill—but in those days it was a hill; developers razed it in 1924. By 1844 the house had 44 inhabitants. As Samuel Brown so rightly wrote, in a letter to his sister in March 1844, "Elizabeth's hands are very full of work . . . what with teaching a class or two, and superintending her household affairs." But that was after the attack.

On that May night in 1843, the Browns were wakened at midnight by loud talking in Chinese outside their window. They assumed it was quarrelling workmen and Samuel Brown shouted out for them to keep quiet. The reverse happened, so he went to the front door. He could see nothing but he soon felt the sharp pain of a spear entering his leg and he shouted out to Elizabeth to get to the henhouse with the children.

Brown himself, losing blood rapidly, grabbed a box of valuables and threw it over the side of the hill before joining his wife in the henhouse where they managed to staunch his wound. The pirates, as they were called for they had come from the sea, vented their frustration at finding nothing of value by breaking down the doors and windows, cutting up the beds and setting fire to piled up clothes.

Elizabeth may have recovered from that ordeal, but her health had been shaky since her arrival in China—the LMS records are dotted with remarks such as the one on 20 January 1841, "We gratefully record the mercy of God in restoring Mrs. Brown to health." The family left Hong Kong on account of Elizabeth's health in 1847.

The next violent robbery to shock Hong Kong was at James White's house in February 1844 and involved his niece Mary Ann Le Foy. The merchant James White, formerly a City of London Alderman, and his family arrived in Hong Kong in October 1843. Edward Cree describes Mary Ann Le Foy as "a nice buxom London girl of 16, a desirable addition to Hong Kong Society". A few days later he dined with them and suggested to his diary, "I make out that Alderman White has lived too fast in

London and has come out on spec & the niece has come out on spec also." Two days later he "Called on Mrs. Alderman White & the blooming niece. Found them very pleasant so put them up to the 'ropes' at Hong Kong." His interest by no means diminished—Cree added on 22 October, "After dinner we called on Mrs. White & her niece, the lovely Mary Ann & brought them off to the *Vixen* & afterwards escorted them home."

Whatever drove the 34-year-old former alderman away from London, he settled quickly in Hong Kong, which was made for men of his kind; he was an expert in silk and had a smooth pen—which he used briefly as editor of *Friend of China;* and he became a Justice of the Peace (JP). The night of the robbery he was away in Shanghai where he was soon to set up in business and make enough money to go back to England and become a Member of Parliament. His wife Mary and Mary Ann were alone in the house.

It is difficult to tell which of Cree's descriptions is

the more evocative, the pictorial one that so appealed to me that I chose it for the front cover, or the verbal one:

Called on Mrs. Alderman White whose house has been broken into by a party of Chinese robbers. She gave a graphic description of the affair and Miss Le Foy added she had 50 Chinamen in her bedroom. That she jumped out of bed & without dressing ran down to the 41st quarters to fetch up the guard. But before she got back the robbers had decamped. Mrs. White did not lose much by the Chinese plunderers, some clothes & nothing of value. Poor Mary Ann lost the clothes she was going to put on—but they had a great fright. These affairs are constantly occuring at Hong Kong where the Chinese are most expert & daring robbers.

IN MARCH 1848, four years later, Cree wrote, "Call on the Misses Hickson & with them to see Mrs. Makrel

Smith, formerly Miss Le Foy, or Poor Mary Ann, who had the 50 Chinese robbers in her room. We had a good laugh over the incident. She is still a very lively young lady." Mary Ann Le Foy disappeared to Shanghai where her husband sold superior pale Sherry, Port and Madeira, and was a broker. No doubt she and Mary Ann Hickson Dale remained friends there.

Some of the incidents could be viewed less philosophically. Cree writes on 8 October 1845, "Some Chinese pirates have been at their old diabolical work. An English blacksmith in the civil engineering department, went home from work and found his wife murdered and house plundered, and the pirates escaped, but hopes are entertained of their capture."

It may be that the situation would have improved with the passage of time and all that meant in terms of the development of law, administration, policing and different cultures getting used to each other, but the so-called 'Lorcha Incident" of October 1856—when a vessel flying the British flag was boarded by Chinese officials—led to a period of incidents between China and Britain, and subsequently to war.

When the British flag was insulted, John Bowring, Governor of Hong Kong, an experienced China hand, oriental scholar and man of peace felt obliged to act militantly. It emerged that Commissioner Yeh, Governor of Kwangtung province, was testing Britain's strength with a view to ridding Canton of the British factories. John Cowper senior was one of the early victims.

The John Cowpers, father and son, had been responsible between 1851 and 1854 for constructing the dry docks at Whampoa, down river from Canton. Thereafter, the father settled with his wife on their chop—the floating, two-storey houseboat ubiquitous in the Pearl River delta. At 5 P.M. on Saturday, 20 December 1856, a sampan came alongside the chop with a letter for Cowper. Husband and wife were walking on the upper deck when their daughter called up to him and he reached out for the letter. As he did so, several men who had been hidden in the sampan lunged at him. Mother and daughter fought frantically to prevent him being pulled overboard, but they failed. Cowper's daughter then jumped into a punt and with the help of two servants tried to follow, but the attack had been well-organized and night was falling; she was forced to give up. On her return to the chop she found her mother lying face downwards and unconscious. It was learnt later that two days after the British opened fire on Canton, Commissioner Yeh issued a proclamation offering 30 silver dollars for every foreign head.

One source says of the Cowpers that "the couple were found murdered in their boat." Austin Coates, in his book *Whampoa* says that old John Cowper "was never seen or heard of again". As for Mrs. Cowper, the impresario Albert Smith met her after the incident, in September 1858, during his three week visit to Hong Kong and Canton. He recorded how he breakfasted on Mr. Cowper's chop, "His mother and sister joined us.

The old lady was very weary of China and longed to be home again."

In order to put pressure on the British, it was also common practice for Chinese authorities on the mainland to manipulate those of its citizens who had flocked to Hong Kong and who served in the early days mainly as servants and coolies. They had done it in Macau, too, and were to continue to do so well into the twentieth century. Usually the result was the withdrawing of labour. In January 1857, however, a more dramatic event aimed at the expatriate population took place. The motive behind the plot to poison all bread eaters (which excluded the Chinese) was never established in a court of law, but its timing coincided with the upset between the two powers.

Fortunately for all concerned, the baker put so much arsenic in the colony's morning bread supply that it acted as an emetic, but many people were very ill that day. No one died then, but it was always maintained that Lady Bowring died the following year as a result of the strain put on her system by the poison. Evidence suggests that both her physical and emotional well-being were already undermined enough to make her, at her age, vulnerable.

Like most of the early governors' wives, Maria Bowring is a shadowy figure, but there are some descriptions of her by George Preble (an American naval officer attached to Commander Perry's expedition to open up Japan, but seconded to the Hong Kong authorities to help in their fight against piracy) which supply some flesh and blood. Research done by her youngest daughter's biographer shows the strain that she may have been under.

Preble met Lady Bowring quite frequently; on 25 February, 1855, he remarked, "I had a pleasant talk with Lady Bowring who is lame, and uses crutches." And in November that year he breakfasted with the Bowrings and noted, "Lady Bowring is very lame, and has been so for seven years. She told me it was with great difficulty she got up and down stairs." The change in weather, then, made no difference to her lameness; in February it is usually cold, grey and very damp; in November it can be crisp, warm, and dry. At Christmas that year—the first Christmas in the new Government House—Preble was among the guests and was again struck by Maria Bowring's disablement but he added, "She told me the other day she was sixty-two years old, just the age of the [American] Commodore [Abbott] at his death. The instant she heard of his death the other day she went in her carriage a mile to tender her sympathy and assistance."

But Maria Bowring, wife of a convinced Unitarian whom she married in 1816 when she was 22, had more to contend with than physical disability. Three of her nine children, including her daughter Emily who was with her in Hong Kong, had become Roman Catholic by 1855. A letter from John Bowring to his son Frederick in 1855 suggests that Emily's parents knew of her conversion in 1853. He refers to a tendency in her towards a "conventual life which to all of us would be eminently repulsive". What is more, Emily's eldest sister, Mary, had already become an

Anglican nun; whether or not she then left holy orders, Mary seems to have been with the family in Hong Kong. There must have been considerable tension within the family which would further undermine Lady Bowring's health. And, as a later chapter shows, war with China and intransigent children were by no means the only worries the Governor, and therefore his wife, had to contend with.

Then on 15 January 1957 Maria Bowring was poisoned. It appears that she was delirious for a time and her husband wrote, "Lady Bowring has been a bad case, as it is thought some arsenic got into her lungs, but the danger is now over." In 1858 she travelled home to England, accompanied by Emily, and she died in Somerset in September. The death certificate gives as the cause, "Ulceration of the stomach—long standing atrophy—4 months certified."

As a result of all the violent incidents of that period, armed Malayan guards were commonplace in the halls of merchant houses, and a host seeing his guests out would buckle on a revolver. A man walking alone outside the city limits by day was quite likely to be mugged. A woman would venture out only in a large party.

Every effort was made to protect Westerners who travelled by boat; in spite of that, a Frenchwoman, Fanny Loviot, was kidnapped when pirates boarded the ship, the *Caldera*, in which she was travelling from Hong Kong in 1854. Ida Pfeiffer, an Australian woman travelling round the world, passed through Hong Kong and Canton in 1847. She could not afford to travel by steamer, so went by Chinese junk to Canton, taking care to put her pistols in order before she did so. Arriving in Canton, she walked boldly through the streets. She noted later, "I was told I might regard it as a quite peculiar piece of good fortune that I had not been grossly insulted and even stoned by the populace."

Women residents, as opposed to those fearlessly passing through, left their houses in Canton only in a closed litter. And even in Hong Kong they must have felt their lives circumscribed. One must be careful, though, not to overemphasize the constraints in Hong Kong: when living in insecure places in insecure times, the only way to survive is to have a fairly relaxed attitude. The light-hearted way that the two Mary Anns looked back on the robbery was more natural than it was insensible. Soon after 1857, too, the news of the horrors of the Indian Mutiny will have reached Hong Kong and people must have felt their little local difficulties rather insignificant. Nevertheless, the strain must sometimes have affected the behavior of women, and men, and their relations with each other.

John le Carré

THE HONOURABLE SCHOOLBOY

A MORE REALISTIC point of departure is a certain typhoon in mid-1974, three o'clock in the afternoon, when Hong Kong lay battened down waiting for the next onslaught. In the bar of the Foreign Correspondents' Club, a score of journalists, mainly from former British colonies—Australian, Canadian, American—fooled and

---

Novelist John le Carré is author of a string of espionage blockbusters, including The Spy Who Came in from the Cold *and* Tinker, Tailor, Soldier, Spy. *His 1977 best-seller,* The Honourable Schoolboy, *follows George Smiley through the mysterious nooks and crannies of underground Hong Kong.*

drank in a mood of violent idleness, a chorus without a hero. Thirteen floors below them, the old trams and double-deckers were caked in the mud-brown sweat of building dust and smuts from the chimney stacks in Kowloon. The tiny ponds outside the high-rise hotels prickled with slow, subversive rain. And in the men's room, which provided the Club's best view of the harbour, young Luke, the Californian, was ducking his face into the handbasin, washing the blood from his mouth.

Luke was a wayward, gangling tennis player, and old man of twenty-seven who, until the American pull-out, had been the star turn in his magazine's Saigon stable of war reporters. When you knew he played tennis, it was hard to think of him doing anything else, even drinking. You imagined him at the net, uncoiling and smashing everything to kingdom come; or serving aces between double faults. His mind, as he sucked and spat, was fragmented by drink and mild concussion—Luke would probably have used the war word "fragged"—into several lucid parts. One part was occupied with a Wanchai bar-girl called Ella, for whose sake had had punched the pig policeman on the jaw and suffered the inevitable consequences. With the minimum necessary force, Superintendent Rockhurst, known otherwise as "the Rocker," who was this minute relaxing in a corner of the bar after his exertions, had knocked Luke cold and kicked him smartly in the ribs. Another part of Luke's mind was on something his Chinese landlord had said to him this morning when he called to complain of the noise of Luke's gramophone, and had stayed to drink a beer.

A scoop of some sort, definitely. But what sort?

He retched again, then peered out of the window. The junks were lashed behind the barriers and the Star Ferry had stopped running. A veteran British frigate lay at anchor, and Club rumours said Whitehall was selling it.

"Should be putting to sea," he muttered confusedly, recalling some bit of naval lore he had picked up in his travels. "Frigates put to sea in typhoons. Yes, *sir.*"

The hills were slate under the stacks of black cloudbanks. Six months ago, the sight would have had him cooing with pleasure. The harbour, the din, even the skyscraper shanties that clambered from the sea's edge upwards to the Peak: after Saigon, Luke had ravenously embraced the whole scene. But all he saw today was a smug, rich British rock run by a bunch of plum-throated traders whose horizons went no farther their their belly-lines. The colony had therefore become for him exactly what it was already for the rest of the journalists: an airfield, a telephone, a laundry, a bed. Occasionally—but never for long—a woman. Where even experience had to be imported. As to the wars which for so long had been his addiction, they were as remote from Hong Kong as they were from London or New York. Only the Stock Exchange showed a token sensibility, and on Saturdays it was closed anyway.

"Think you're going to live, ace?" asked the shaggy Canadian cowboy, coming to the stall beside him. The two men had shared the pleasures of the Tet offensive.

"Thank you, dear, I feel perfectly topping," Luke replied, in his most exalted English accent.

Luke decided it really was important for him to remember what Jake Chiu had said to him over the beer this morning, and suddenly, like a gift from heaven, it came to him.

"I remember!" he shouted. "Jesus, cowboy, I remember! Luke, you remember! My brain! It works! Folks, give ear to Luke!"

"Forget it," the cowboy advised. "That's badland out there today, ace. Whatever it is, forget it."

But Luke kicked open the door and charged into the bar, arms flung wide.

"Hey! Hey! *Folks!*"

Not a head turned. Luke cupped his hands to his mouth.

"Listen, you drunken bums, I got *news*. This is fantastic. Two bottles of Scotch a day and a brain like a razor. Someone give me a bell."

Finding none, he grabbed a tankard and hammered it on the bar rail, spilling beer. Even then, only the dwarf paid him the slightest notice.

"So what's happened, Lukie?" whined the dwarf, in his queeny Greenwich Village drawl. "Has Big Moo gotten hiccups again? I can't bear it."

Big Moo was Club jargon for the Governor, and the dwarf was Luke's chief of bureau. He was a pouchy, sullen creature, with disordered hair that wept in black strands over his face, and a silent way of popping up beside you. A year back, two Frenchmen, otherwise rarely seen there, had nearly killed him for a chance remark he had made on the origins of the mess in Vietnam. They took him to the lift, broke his jaw and several of his ribs, then dumped him in a heap on the ground floor and came back to finish their drinks. Soon afterwards the Australians did a similar job on him when he made a silly accusation about their token military involvement in the war. He suggested that Canberra had done a deal with President Johnson to keep the Australian boys in Vung Tau, which was a picnic, while the Americans did the real fighting elsewhere. Unlike the French, the Australians didn't even bother to use the 'lift. They just beat the hell out of the dwarf where he stood, and when he fell they added a little more of the same. After that, he learned to keep clear of certain people in Hong Kong. In times of persistent fog, for instance. Or when the water was cut to four hours a day. Or on a typhoon Saturday.

Otherwise the Club was pretty much empty. For reasons of prestige, the top correspondents steered clear of the place anyway. A few businessmen, who came for the flavour pressmen give; a few girls, who came for the men. A couple of war tourists in fake battledrill. And in his customary corner, the awesome Rocker, Superintendent of Police, ex-Palestine, ex-Kenya, ex-Malaya, ex-Fiji, and implacable war-horse, with a beer, one set of slightly reddened knuckles, and a weekend copy of the *South China Morning Post.* The Rocker, people said, came for the class.

At the big table at the centre, which on weekdays was the preserve of United Press International, lounged the Shanghai Junior Baptist Conservative Bowling Club, presided over by mottled old Craw, the Australian, enjoying its usual Saturday tournament. The aim of the contest was to pitch a screwed-up napkin across the room and lodge it in the wine rack. Every time you succeeded, your competitors bought you the bottle and helped you drink it. Old Craw growled the orders to fire, and an elderly Shanghainese waiter, Craw's favourite, wearily manned the butts and served the prizes. The game was not a zestful one that day, and some members were not bothering to throw. Nevertheless this was the group Luke selected for his audience.

"Big Moo's *wife's* got hiccups!" the dwarf insisted. "Big Moo's wife's *horse* has got hiccups! Bit Moo's wife's horse's *groom's* got hiccups! Big Moo's wife's horse's——"

Striding to the table, Luke leapt straight onto it with a crash, breaking several glasses and cracking his head on the ceiling in the process. Framed up there against the south window in a half-crouch, he was out of scale to everyone: the dark mist, the dark shadow of the Peak behind it, and this giant filling the whole foreground. But they went on pitching and drinking as if they hadn't seen him. Only the Rocker glanced in Luke's direction, once, before licking a huge thumb and turning to the cartoon page.

"Round three," Craw ordered, in his rich Australian accent. "Brother Canada, prepare to fire. *Wait*, you slob. Fire."

A screwed-up napkin floated toward the rack, taking a high trajectory. Finding a cranny, it hung a moment, then flopped to the ground. Egged on by the dwarf, Luke began stamping on the table and more glasses fell. Finally he wore his audience down.

"Your Graces," said old Craw, with a sigh. "Pray silence for my son. I fear he would have parley with us. Brother Luke, you have committed several acts of war today and one more will meet with our severe disfavour. Speak clearly and concisely omitting no detail, however slight, and thereafter hold your water, sir."

In their tireless pursuit of legends about one another, old Craw was their Ancient Mariner. Craw had shaken more sand out of his shorts, they told each other, than most of them would walk over; and they were right. In Shanghai, where his career had started, he had been teaboy and city editor to the only English-speaking journal in the port. Since then, he had covered the Communists against

Chiang Kai-shek and Chiang against the Japanese and the Americans against practically everyone. Craw gave them a sense of history in this rootless place. His style of speech, which at typhoon times even the hardiest might pardonably find irksome, was a genuine hangover from the thirties, when Australia provided the bulk of journalists in the Orient, and the Vatican, for some reason, the jargon of their companionship.

So Luke, thanks to old Craw, finally got it out.

"Gentlemen! Dwarf, you damn Polack, let go of my foot! Gentlemen." He paused to dab his mouth with a handkerchief. "The house known as High Haven is for sale and His Grace Tufty Thesinger has flown the coop."

Nothing happened, but he didn't expect much anyway. Journalists are not given to cries of amazement or even incredulity.

"High Haven," Luke repeated sonorously, "is up for grabs. Mr. Jake Chiu, the well-known and popular real-estate entrepreneur, more familiar to you as my personal irate landlord, has been charged by Her Majesty's majestic government to *dispose* of High Haven. To wit, peddle. Let me go, you Polish bastard, I'll kill you!"

The dwarf had toppled him. Only a flailing, agile leap saved him from injury. From the floor, Luke hurled more abuse at his assailant. Meanwhile, Craw's large head had turned to Luke, and his moist eyes fixed on him a baleful stare that seemed to go on forever. Luke began to wonder which of Craw's many laws he might have sinned against. Beneath his various disguises, Craw was a complex and solitary figure, as everyone round the table knew. Under the willed roughness of his manner lay a love of the East which seemed sometimes to string him tighter than he could stand, so that there were months when he would disappear from sight altogether and, like a sulky elephant, go off on his private paths until he was once more fit to live with.

"Don't burble, Your Grace, do you mind?" said Craw at last, and tilted back his big head imperiously. "Refrain from spewing low-grade bilge into highly salubrious water, will you, Squire? High Haven's the spookhouse. Been the spookhouse for years. Lair of the lynx-eyed Major Tufty Thesinger, formerly of Her Majesty's Rifles, presently Hong Kong's Lestrade of the Yard. Tufty wouldn't fly the coop. He's a hood, not a tit. Give my son a drink, Monsignor:"—this to the Shanghainese barman—"he's wandering."

Craw intoned another fire order and the Club returned to its intellectual pursuits. The truth was, there was little new to these great spy scoops by Luke. He had a long reputation as a failed spookwatcher, and his leads were invariably disproved. Since Vietnam, the stupid lad saw spies under every carpet. He believed the world was run by them, and much of his spare time, when he was sober, was spent hanging round the Colony's numberless battalions of thinly disguised China-watchers, and worse, who infested the enormous American Consulate up the hill. So if it hadn't been such a listless day, the matter would probably have rested there. As it was, the dwarf saw an opening to amuse, and seized it.

"Tell us, Lukie," he suggested, with a queer upward twisting of the hands, "are they selling High Haven with *contents* or *as found?*"

The question won him a round of applause. Was High Haven worth more with its secrets or without?

"Do they sell it with *Major Thesinger?*" the South African photographer pursued, in his humourless singsong, and there was more laughter still, though it was no more affectionate. The photographer was a disturbing figure, crew cut and starved, and his complexion was pitted like the battlefields he loved to haunt. He came from Cape Town, but they called him Deathwish the Hun. The saying way, he would bury all of them, for he stalked them like a mute.

For several diverting minutes now, Luke's point was lost entirely under a spate of Major Thesinger stories and Major Thesinger imitations, in which all but Craw joined. It was recalled that the Major had made his first appearance in the Colony as an importer, with some fatuous cover down among the docks; only to transfer, six months later, quite improbably, to the services' list and, complete with his staff of pallid clerks and doughy, well-bred secretaries, decamp to the said spookhouse as somebody's replacement.

In particular, the Major's *tête-à-tête* luncheons were described, to which, as it now turned out, practically every journalist listening had at one time or another been invited. And which ended with laborious proposals over brandy, including such wonderful phrases as: "Now, look here, old man, if you should ever bump into an interesting Chow from over the river, you know—one with *access*, follow me?—just you remember High Haven!" Then the magic telephone number—the one that "rings spot on my desk, no middle men, tape-recorders, nothing, right?" which a good half-dozen of them seemed to have in their diaries: "Here, pencil this one on your cuff; pretend it's a date or a girl-friend or something. Ready for it? Hong Kong-side five zero two four . . ."

Having chanted the five digits in unison, they fell quiet. Somewhere a clock chimed for three-fifteen. Luke slowly stood up and brushed the dust from his jeans. The old Shanghainese waiter gave up his post by the racks and reached for the menu, in the hope that someone might eat. For a moment, uncertainty overcame them. The day was forfeit. It had been so since the first gin.

In the background, a low grown sounded as the Rocker ordered himself a generous luncheon: "And bring me a cold beer, *cold*, you hear, boy? *Muchee coldee. Chop chop.*" The Superintendent had his way with natives and said this every time. The quiet returned.

"Well, there you are, Lukie," the dwarf called, moving

away. "That's how you win your Pulitzer, I guess. Congratulations, darling. Scoop of the year."

"Ah, go impale yourselves, the bunch of you," said Luke carelessly and started to make his way down the bar to where two sallow blond girls sat, army daughters on the prowl. "Jake Chiu showed me the damned letter of instruction, didn't he? On her Majesty's damn Service, wasn't it? Damn crest on the top, lion screwing a goat. Hi, sweethearts, remember me? I'm the kind man who bought you the lollipops at the fair."

"Thesinger don't answer." Deathwish the Hun sang mournfully from the telephone. "Nobody don't answer. Not Thesinger, not his duty man. They disconnected the line." In the excitement, or the monotony, no one had noticed Deathwish slip away.

TILL NOW, OLD Craw the Australian had lain dead as a dodo. Now he looked up sharply.

"Dial it again, you fool," he ordered, tart as a drill sergeant.

With a shrug, Deathwish dialed Thesinger's number a second time, and a couple of them went to watch him do it. Craw stayed put, watching from where he sat. There were two instruments. Deathwish tried the second, but with no better result.

"Ring the operator," Craw ordered across the room to them. "Don't stand there like a pregnant banshee. Ring the operator, you African ape!"

Number disconnected, said the operator.

"Since when, man?" Deathwish demanded, into the mouthpiece.

No information available, said the operator.

"Maybe they got a new number then, right man?" Deathwish howled, still at the luckless operator. No one had ever seen him so involved. Life for Deathwish was what happened at the end of a viewfinder: such passion was only attributable to the typhoon.

No information available, said the operator.

"Ring Shallow Throat," Craw ordered, now quite furious. "Ring every damned striped-pants in the Colony!"

Deathwish shook his long head uncertainly. Shallow Throat was the official government spokesman, a hate object to them all. To approach him for anything was bad face.

"Here, give him to me," said Craw and, rising to his feet, shoved them aside to get to the phone and embark on the lugubrious courtship of Shallow Throat. "Your devoted Craw, sir, at your service. How's Your Eminence in mind and health? Charmed, sir, charmed. And the wife and beg, sir? All eating well, I trust? No scurvy or typhus? Good. Well now, perhaps you'll have the benison to advise me why the hell Tufty Thesinger's flown the coop?"

They watched him, but his face had set like rock, and there was nothing more to read there.

"And the same to you, sir!" he snorted finally, and slammed the phone back on its cradle so hard the whole table bounced. Then he turned to the old Shanghainese waiter. "Monsignor Goh, sir, order me a petrol donkey and oblige! Your Graces, get off your arses, the pack of you!"

"What the hell for?" said the dwarf, hoping to be included in the command.

"For a story, you snotty little Cardinal, for a story, Your lecherous, alcoholic Eminences. For wealth, fame, women, and longevity!"

"But what did Shallow Throat say that was so damn bad?" the shaggy Canadian cowboy asked, mystified.

The dwarf echoed him. "Yeah, so what did he say, Brother Craw?"

"He said, 'No comment,'" Craw replied with fine dignity, as if the words were the vilest slur upon his professional honour.

So up the Peak they went, leaving only the silent majority of drinkers to their peace: restive Deathwish the Hun went, long Luke, then the shaggy Canadian cowboy, very striking in his Mexican revolutionary moustache, the dwarf, attaching as ever, and finally old Craw and the two army girls—a plenary session of the Shanghai Junior Baptist Conservative Bowling Club, therefore, with ladies added, though the Club was sworn to celibacy. Amazingly, the jolly Cantonese driver took them all, a triumph of exuberance of physics. He even consented to give three receipts for the full fare, one for each of the journals represented, a thing no Hong Kong taxi-driver had been known to do before or since. It was a day to break all precedents. Old Craw sat in the front wearing his famous soft straw hat with Eton colours on the ribbon, bequeathed to him by an old comrade in his will. The dwarf was squeezed over the gear lever, the other three men sat in the back, and the two girls sat on Luke's lap, which made it hard for him to dab his mouth.

The Rocker did not see fit to join them. He had tucked his napkin into his collar in preparation for the Club's roast lamb and mint sauce and a lot of potatoes: "And another beer! But *cold* this time—hear that, boy? *Muchee coldee,* and bring it *chop chop.*"

But once the coast was clear, the Rocker also made use of the telephone, and spoke to Someone in Authority, just to be on the safe side, though they agreed there was nothing to be done.

THE TAXI WAS a red Mercedes, quite new, but nowhere kills a car faster than the Peak, climbing at no speed forever, air-conditioners at full blast. The weather continued awful. As the car sobbed slowly up the concrete cliffs, they were engulfed by a fog thick enough to choke on. When they got out, it was even worse. A hot, unbudgeable curtain had spread itself across the summit, reeking of petrol and crammed with the din of the valley.

The moisture floated in hot fine swarms. On a clear day they would have had a view both ways, one of the loveliest on earth: northward to Kowloon and the blue mountains of the New Territories, which hid from sight the eight hundred million Chinese who lacked the privilege of British rule; southward to Repulse and Deep Water Bays and the open China Sea. High Haven, after all, had been built by the Royal Navy in the twenties in all the grand innocence of that service, to receive and impart a sense of power.

But that afternoon, if the house had not been set among the trees, and in a hollow where the trees grew tall in their efforts to reach the sky, and if the trees had not kept the fog out, they would have had nothing to look at but the two white concrete pillars—one bearing bell buttons marked "DAY" and "NIGHT"—and the chained gates they supported. Thanks to the trees, however, they saw the house clearly, though it was set back fifty yards. They could pick out the drain-pipes, fire-escapes, and washing lines and they could admire the green dome which the Japanese army had added during their four years' tenancy.

Hurrying to the front in his desire to be accepted, the dwarf pressed the bell marked "DAY." A speaker was let into the pillar and they all stared at it, waiting for it to say something or, as Luke would have it, puff out pot-smoke. At the roadside, the Cantonese driver had switched on his radio full, and it was playing a whining Chinese love song, on and on. The second pillar was blank except for a brass plate announcing the Inter Services Liaison Staff, Thesinger's threadbare cover. Deathwish the Hun had produced a camera and was photographing as methodically as if he were on one of his native battlefields.

"Maybe they don't work Saturdays," Luke suggested while they continued to wait, at which Craw told him not to be bloody silly; spooks worked seven days a week and round the clock, he said. Also they never ate, apart from Tufty.

"*Good* afternoon to you," said the dwarf.

Pressing the night bell, he had put his twisted red lips to the vents of the speaker and affected an upper-class English accent, which, to give him credit, he managed surprisingly well.

"My name is Michael Hanbury-Steadly-Heamoor, and I'm personal bumboy to Big Moo. I should like *pliss*, to speak to Major Thesinger on a matter of some urgency, *pliss*. There is a mushroom-shaped cloud the Major may not have noticed; it *appearce* to be forming over the *Pearl* River and it's spoiling Big Moo's golf. *Thenk* you. Will you kindly open the gate?"

One of the blond girls gave a titter.

"I didn't know he was a *Steadly*-Heamoor," she said.

Abandoning Luke, they had tethered themselves to the shaggy Canadian's arm, and spent a lot of time whispering in his ear.

"He's Rasputin," said one of the girls admiringly,

stroking the back of his thigh. "I've seen the film. He's the spitten image, aren't you, Canada?"

Now everybody had a drink from Luke's flask while they regrouped and wondered what to do. From the direction of the parked cab, the driver's Chinese love song .continued dauntlessly, but the speakers on the pillars said nothing at all. The dwarf pressed both bells at once, and tried an Al Capone threat.

"Now see here, Thesinger, we know you're in there. You come out with your hands raised, uncloaked, throw down your dagger—*Hey, watch it, you stupid cow!*"

The imprecation was addressed neither to the Canadian nor to old Craw—who was sidling toward the trees, apparently to meet a call of nature—but to Luke, who had decided to beat his way into the house. The gateway stood in a muddy service bay sheltered by dripping trees. On the far side was a pile of refuse, some new. Sauntering over to this in search of an illuminating clue, Luke had unearthed a piece of pig-iron made in the shape of an "S." Having carted it to the gate, though it must have weighed thirty pounds or more, he was holding it two-handed above his head and driving it against the staves, at which the gate tolled like a cracked bell.

Deathwish had sunk to one knee, his hollowed face clawed into a martyr's smile as he shot.

"Counting five, Tufty!" Luke yelled, with another shat-tering heave. "One . . ." He struck again. "Two . . ."

Overhead an assorted flock of birds, some very large, lifted out of the trees and flew in slow spirals, but the thunder of the valley and the boom of the gate drowned their screams. The taxi-driver was dancing about, clapping and laughing, his love song forgotten. Stranger still, in view of the menacing weather, an entire Chinese family appeared, pushing not one pram but two, and they began laughing, also—even the smallest child—holding their hands across their mouths to conceal their teeth. Till suddenly the

Canadian cowboy let out a cry, shook off the girls, and pointed through the gates.

"For Lord's sake, what the heck's Craw doing? Old Buzzard's jumped the wire."

By now, whatever sense or normal scale there might have been had vanished. A collective madness had seized everyone. The drink, the black day, the claustrophobia had gone to their heads entirely. The girls fondled the Canadian with abandon, Luke continued his hammering, the Chinese were hooting with laughter, until with divine timeliness the fog lifted, temples of blue-black cloud soared directly above them, and a torrent of rain crashed into the trees. A second longer and it hit them, drenching them in the first swoop. The girls, suddenly half naked, flew laughing and shrieking for the Mercedes, but the male ranks held firm—even the dwarf held firm—staring through the films of water at the unmistakable figure of the old Australian in his Etonian hat, standing in the shelter of the house under a rough porch that looked as if it were made for bicycles, though no one but a lunatic would bicycle up the Peak.

"Craw! they screamed. "Monsignor! The bastard's scooped us!"

The din of the rain was deafening; the branches seemed to be cracking under its force. Luke had thrown aside his mad hammer. The shaggy cowboy went first, Luke and the dwarf followed, Deathwish with his smile and his camera brought up the tail, crouching and hobbling as he continued photographing blindly. The rain poured off them as it wanted, sloshing in red rivulets round their ankles as they pursued Craw's trail up a slope where the screech of bullfrogs added to the row. They scaled a bracken ridge, slithered to a halt before a barbed-wire fence, clambered through the parted strands, and crossed a low ditch. By the time they reached him, Craw was gazing at the green cupola, while the rain—despite the straw hat—ran busily off his jaw, turning his trim fawn suit into a blackened, shapeless tunic. He stood as if mesmerised, staring upward.

Luke, who loved him best, spoke first. "Your Grace? Hey, wake up! It's me—Romeo. Jesus Christ, what the hell's eating him?"

Suddenly concerned, Luke gently touched his arm. But still Craw didn't speak.

"Maybe he died standing up," the dwarf suggested, while grinning Deathwish photographed him on this happy off chance.

Like an old prize-fighter, Craw slowly rallied. "Brother Luke, we owe you a handsome apology, sir," he muttered.

"Get him back to the cab," said Luke, and began clearing a way for him, but the old boy refused to move.

"Tufty Thesinger. A good scout. Not a flyer—not sly enough for flight—but a good scout."

"Tufty Thesinger rest in peace," said Luke impatiently.

"Let's go. Dwarf, move your ass."

"He's stoned," said the cowboy.

"Consider the clues, Watson," Craw resumed, after another pause for meditation, while Luke tugged at his arm and the rain came on still faster. "Remark first the empty cages over the window, whence air-conditioners have been untimely ripped. Parsimony, my son, a commendable virtue—especially, if I may say so, in a spook. Notice the dome there? Study it carefully, sir. Scratch marks. Not, alas, the footprints of a gigantic hound, but the scratch marks of wireless aerials removed by the frantic hand of round-eyes. Ever heard of a spookhouse without a wifeless aerial? Might as well have a cathouse without a piano."

The rainfall had reached a crescendo. Huge drops thumped around them like shot. Craw's face was a mix of things Luke could only guess at. Deep in his heart it occurred to him that Craw really might be dying. Luke had seen little of natural death, and was very much on the alert for it.

"Maybe they just got rock-fever and split," he said, trying again to coax him to the car.

"Very possibly, Your Grace, very possibly indeed. It is certainly the season for rash, ungovernable acts."

"Home," said Luke, and pulled firmly at his arm. "Make a path there, will you? Stretcher party."

But the old man still lingered stubbornly for a last look at the English spookhouse flinching in the storm.

R. C. Hurley

HANDBOOK TO HONGKONG

THE BRITISH CROWN Colony of Hongkong with its latest acquired dependencies is the most interesting Port of Call for Visitors to the Far East, as it is also the most important commercial and shipping centre in this part of the world.

It comprises the Island of Hongkong, the Kowloon Peninsula (3 sq. miles since 1860) and the New

R.C. Hurley was a frequent traveler to Hong Kong in the early 1900's. In 1920, he assembled the ultimate tour guide: Handbook to the British Crown Colony of Hongkong and Dependencies. *These excerpts are typical of the guide—filled with everything a traveling Britisher would need to know, from Hygiene tips to correct dress for Shooting.*

Territories (300 sq. miles since 1899) of the adjacent Sun-On District together with numerous islands in the vicinity including the larger island of Lan-tao with its lofty twin peaks, Tai-u-shan.

The topographical attractions of this area are exceptional in character, yielding magnificent views of both land and sea scapes in every direction: range upon range of hills and mountains—mostly verdure-clad—with some of their peaks attaining to the respectable altitude of over 3,000 feet above the sea-level.

The surrounding waterways are equally beautiful—in one of the finest harbours to be found anywhere in the world—which affords safe anchorage for any and all Naval and Mercantile Marine Shipping entering and making use of the port. Originally a free port (up to August, 1914), there are certain restrictions and formalities now in force.

Within this extensive harbour and around the Island to the south will be discovered many pretty bays and inlets which offer splendid fishing and bathing facilities, magnificent beaches and well-wooded picnic shelters—all that can possibly be desired; in fact, every pleasure that outdoor life and exercise affords, including yachting and aquatic sports generally—on a grand scale—can be had in Hongkong almost for the asking.

Walking and hill-climbing, cycling and motoring for all who reside at a distance from town are, as a rule, part of the daily routine.

And again, a special feature for those who feel the heat during the summer: a complete change of climate can be enjoyed within easy distance of the lower levels by a trip on the funicular railway up to the terminus at Victoria Gap, some 1,200 feet above sea-level, the temperature being from 10 to 15 degrees lower than the town according to direction of wind and humidity.

There is no place in the Far East where, with so little expenditure of both time and money, such health-offering advantages can be as readily secured, as in the British Crown Colony of Hongkong.

The capital city of Hongkong is Victoria, which

occupies the northern shore of the island for a stretch of about four miles and extends for nearly 600 feet up the side of the mountain.

The Peak District above, where a great many handsome residences have been built with easy approach from a well laid out system of mountain roads, covers quite an extensive area and is much appreciated as a summer resort by dwellers in the city below and from the neighboring outports.

Looking south from the deck of a mail steamer moored away in the harbour, the prospect is one of surprise and admiration. Tier upon tier of substantially-built terraces, spacious homes and costly mansions rising one above another until precipitous ascent precludes the possibility of further sites for building. This same prospect reviewed at night under a cloudy sky, when the city is lit up with myriads of electric lights, becomes a dazzling spectacle indeed long to be remembered.

To reverse the picture. Looking north from Victoria Gap or the Signal Station at the Peak: the intensive panorama over the harbour crowded with shipping, native and foreign, and away beyond the original Kowloon boundary will be seen a range of high hills stretching for about thirty miles from east to west, with its loftiest peak, Tai-mo-shan, ten miles distant in the centre. Beyond this range, approached over the frontier or Tai-po Road and quite within an hour of the City of Victoria, will be found the most interesting and fertile Sha-tin Valley, noted for its special cultivation of fine white rice formerly commandeered for the Royal Palaces at Peking. This valley at harvest time, from early June to late October (3 crops) when most of the villagers are out in the rice-fields, gives a charming picture of peasant life in this part of the Flowery Land.

In the near distance is seen the Tide Cove, an arm of a miniature inland sea to all appearances a perfectly land-locked and self-contained area of something like thirty square miles girt in by many a picturesque mountainous group.

Among these hills in their ravines and in their waterways will be found a variety of interests. For the botanist any number of indigenous flowering trees and shrubs, a beautiful flora with many specimens of the wild orchid and, on their lower slopes, ingeniously irrigated patches of soil in terraces on which the natives grow their rice and vegetables.

There is yet another attraction of no mean order for those who are prepared to look Dame Fortune straight in the face without blushing: geological survey describes the formation of the country as "highly mineralised" *in certain sections,* there being at the same time an accumulation of faults, which means may be undreamt of possibilities for the man who has the patience to devote himself persever-ingly to discovery.

As regards fauna, among the groups of boulders and in some of the thicker undergrowth, small packs of jackals may occasionally be seen making off when disturbed, at a great pace; foxes also and several smaller kinds of the feline species, one of them quite a big specimen. . . . But, under a full harvest moon when the weird lighting effect on these great masses of rock produces a veritable land of hobgoblins fit for Oberon, one has to beware of the possible presence of the living fairy queen "Stripes" as every fall season she is known to make occasional nocturnal visits to this highly interesting locality in search of a sumptuous repast—pig, deer, goat, or dog—without payment.

HYGIENE

Hints on Rational Living in Hongkong (Forty years' experience)

IN NEARLY ALL hot climates the most refreshing hour is that at dawn of day, when the heat rays of the sun have been absent for many hours.

RISE AT DAYBREAK.—Salt-water gargle.

FORMULA.—A teaspoonful of table salt dissolved in sufficient boiling water to fill a white quart bottle, decant when cold. The first thing on rising, gargle for one minute. A little later a tumbler of warm water followed by fruit, bananas for preference, oranges also in season.

DRESS IN FLANNELS.—Take at least forty minutes easy walk which means 2 miles (5,000) paces, long enough to set all physical and mental machinery in healthy motion—returning before the heat of the sun is felt.

BATH.—Cold shower with mild carbolic soap, to be completed with exertion in one minute. Free use of rough towel, etc., dress according to season—never too heavy.

BREAKFAST.—At 7.30 if possible. Fresh ripe fruit, or prunes stewed with oranges, followed by a farinaceous dish with fresh milk. Fish or hot bacon with eggs, ham and the usual Colds. Watercress during the winter season.

Nothing between meals and no superfluous drinking—a glass of water will prove the safest lubricant.

TIFFIN.—At 12.30 if possible, according to habit and appetite, the lighter the better to avoid any feeling of drowsiness afterwards.

DINNER.—Dinner should be taken as soon after 6.30 p.m. as convenient, allowing time for an hour's stroll afterwards; conducive to sleep and freshness on rising in the morning.

NIGHT CAP.—On retiring a tumbler of warm water.

HEAD REST.—The Chinese *Chum-tow* which takes up

only one-thirtieth the space of the ordinary feather or flock pillow, will afford a much freer air-circulation for breathing purposes, is more comfortable and highly recommended as conducive to sleep.

Outfit Necessary for Shooting and Walking Trips

As these trips will not exceed more than a few days, no great preparation need be made as if for a lengthened stay.

RAILWAY to Fanling or to Lo-Fu Ferry.

BOAT.—Steam launch and or Hakka-boat with small punt or dinghy sailing (on the first of the flood-tide when leaving Hongkong) round to Deep Bay River.

DRESS.—(Mufti) Seasonable according to duration of trip. Sun-topey indispensible (flannels recommended.)

COMMISSARIAT.—Hongkong filtered water, bread, biscuits, butter, cheese, cooked fresh meat and *Dairy Farm Pork Pies*, tinned milk, potatos, preserves, tea, coffee, sugar, salt and a cruet. Bananas and other fruits in season.

LIGHT.—Tea-oil lamps, candles and matches.

SPORTING GEAR.—Fowling-piece, duck-gun and revolver,—with a big-game rifle during the mid-autumn season—ammunition for all.

RECREATION.—Cards, reading-matter, cigarettes, cigars and tobacco.

PERSONAL.—Medicines and liquors. A good stout walking stick.

SCIENTIFIC.—Pocket aneroid, compass and pedometer. Testing hammer and glass.

George Adams

A NIGHT IN CHUNG KING

THE SIGN, SCRAWLED in blue ink marker on a large white board, read:

> IT IS STRICTLY FOBIDDEN FOR ANY
> BODY TO THROW THEIR GABAGES OR
> ABANTONE SUCH AS CARTON BOXES OR

British writer George Adams is the author of several amusing satires of life in Hong Kong, including Games Hong Kong People Play *and* A Social Psychology of the Hong Kong Chinese. *"A Night in Chung King" is from his latest collection,* Wicked Hong Kong Stories *(1992). Adams lives in Kowloon.*

FURNITURES IN THE PUBIC AREA.

THOSE ILLEGALITY WILL BE LEGA-
LLY PRONCUTED.

FOR THOSE GABAGES PLEASE DE-
LIVER TO THE GABAGE COLLECTION STA-
TION WHICH IS AT THE VREAR DOOR
G/F BLOCK B OF THE SHOPPING ARCADE.

CHUN KING MANSION ADMINISTR-
ATIVE OFFICE 21 MAY 1992

IT WAS ATTACHED to one of the pillars on the stifling first floor of the decrepit rabbit warren of a building
in the middle of Tsim Sha Tsui known as Chung King
Mansion. Morris had spotted it on his first tour of the
place that afternoon, on his stopover from Australia—the
final stopover, he hoped. The sign looked a great deal like

some of the telex messages that used to arrive in the old days: ACTRESS KILLED BY DRINK AND RUGS or POLICEMAN SHAT IN ROBBERY ATTEMPT.

Morris, a small, wiry man in his early sixties, could hardly breathe when he stopped walking. The sweat could not ooze out of him fast enough, the healthy sweat of the perspiring anybody and the extra supply brought on by Old Jim Beam. Next to him, also looking at the sign, stood a young Indian gentleman in collar and tie and a three-piece suit without, Morris noticed, more than a token bead of perspiration on his furrowed brow.

"It is very funny when I look at it again. The queen would be shocked by such English," the Indian gentleman said. Morris smiled and focused on the man's intelligent face through his thick lenses.

"Quite."

He then shuffled off towards the narrow staircase, passing the restaurant touts on the way to the fag shop. He had bought a pack on his way in. That had been that morning and as usual they had dwindled down to a few broken ones. He always broke a few when he hit the bottle and he had to have a decent session that day.

Morris had covered some sheep stations and queer houses in his time as a reporter but Chung King was a revelation. From the Chinese world of bustling Nathan Road one entered into the Black Hole of Calcutta via Arabian Nights and the Taj Mahal. The transformation was radical. Curry took over from the gasoline in the air, costumes changed from the conservative Chinese suits to turbans, gowns and thongs; the Golden Mile became a bazaar. Morris half expected Bob Hope and Dorothy Lamour to appear around the corner or to be offered dirty postcards by a ragamuffin Moorish boy. The boy might even offer himself . . .

Seated on a rickety stool in the disgusting restaurant at the back of the arcade, Morris peeled the cellophane wrapper from the red Dunhill pack with sensual delight. His accompanying tremor was not one of excitement.

Nowadays, he had difficulty with the keys of his baby Olympia typewriter. That had been the beginning of the end. Everything took that much longer. The boss had let him go with a generous cheque. It had only taken him fifteen minutes to leave. So few had noticed he had gone. In his small room in Foote Street, there had been very little to pack, very little anyone would want to hang on to if the bottom had dropped out of his life. One suitcase full of his worn suits and dated underwear, one small attaché case containing principally his typewriter, the pills and, of course, the manuscript. There were also very few friends left to say goodbye to. So many had moved up the coast, passed away, moved on as it were. The pubs were unrecognisable, hasty places with fast food and piped music. Get in, consume and get out. What was the point of hanging on? The flights to Hong Kong were quite cheap, if you didn't mind knees up the nose class all the way. From there, he had thought of dropping in on his brother in England to see what he could do for him. There had to be something he could do. But that plan, like so many, had faded before it could take shape.

Just then, the fear came back to him. He sipped the brown, creamy tea before him in a thick plastic cup on top of the collapsible Formica table, feeling like a little boy again on his first day at school. The hands quivered as he opened the newspaper he had found lightly sticking to the table. It was one of the local English rags, actually quite nicely done, as good as his own paper in Australia in some respects but with too much syndicated stuff. Must be understaffed. He noticed the telephone number at the top of the page. Perhaps they might need a copy editor.

But no, he would never work again after today. He would not breathe again, after today.

Once more, Morris was being grinned at, this time by a particularly fat and repulsive Indian seated at the same table.

"Good evening, sir. Where you from? Australia? England? I see. Need some clothes? I have some very nice silk garments in stock. Suits I can do for you in twelve hours no trouble and what about some leather jackets? Special discount."

It was impossible to avoid the touts. At almost every corner, on every staircase they hovered, insistent, impervious to satire or denial. The best tactic was simply to ignore them. Morris left the relative cool of the cafe and made his way to the elevator lobby. Monochrome images of lift interiors flickered on clapped-out mini-monitors above the ground floor entrance. The people in the lift, displayed televisually, looked like startled astronauts. There were many rucksack people waiting to go to the Berlin Hotel or the Texas Lodge, just two of the hundreds of flop-houses which went under the name of hotel in Chung King. They were all fire traps and insect zoos.

Morris entered block F lift, squeezing himself

between an unshaven Swiss or German he thought, to judge by his guttural language. The man was in heated discussion with an attractive but slovenly blonde girl. Both were dressed in Afghan or Kashmiri clothes complete with sequined hat and sandals. Neither looked out of place. No one but a local Chinese looked out of place in Chung King. A huge Indian—Morris had not seen a thin one in Chung King so far apart from Mr. Daswani—stood behind him wafting an indescribably complex odour of sweat, cumin, cologne and smoke onto him. The lift, Morris thought, was impossibly small to serve the people who lived in the block.

The Balmoral Raj Guest House and Tandoori Kitchen (We Also Serve Full English Breakfast) was hidden behind a lace-curtained glass door and Morris knew why it was hidden. If a potential guest could glimpse inside, he would never enter. Once through the door, however, under the persuasive charm of Mr. Daswani and his niece, very few weary travellers would summon

the rightness of the decision. But how to lead up to the inevitable? That needed some thought.

He would simply buy the best meal of his life, spend some time with a woman (boys were so unsubstantial in Hong Kong), buy a cigar (he really hated the things) and then, around midnight, take the pills. He had the note ready to make things easy for Mr. Daswani. There was a cheque to cover the funeral expenses and instructions for the manuscript. He was particularly concerned about the five hundred pages of novel he had composed over the last twenty years, much of it whilst drunk. The muses had always appeared to be at their most inspirational when he was well-oiled.

Morris took another swig of *Highland Heather,* a brew he liked and which he had not seen in Australia for years. Hong Kong simply had everything, it seemed. Descending in the lift, he was in a delicious reverie about his first years as a reporter, covering society weddings and soccer matches on wet Saturday afternoons. It was probably then that he had been at his happiest, before the boozing started, before he had met Julie, the woman who in the end had refused to become his wife . . .

He had to get out of Chung King. Perhaps his budget might extend to a night in the Hyatt as well as his last treats? No, it wouldn't. Besides the money he had saved for his final days in Hong Kong, he was penniless. The months of no work, his moping in Foote Street, his boozy afternoons in the park, the boys he had desperately brought home with him, it had all eaten into his savings. Fortunately, he had bought the ticket early on, before his brother had ruled out any real help in his (so appallingly badly-written!) first communication in twenty-three years.

Running the gauntlet of the copy watch touts, Morris made his way to what, in his guide, looked like Kowloon Park. He climbed the steep stairs at the entrance with some difficulty and felt his heart beating harder than he had known it to for some time. The air, which had been stifling, was cooling slightly in the early evening. People did not look as frenetic as they had done at the airport, pushing past him at every turn, refusing to budge from their steady collision course until the last possible moment. The locals were not always short-sighted boors, it appeared, at least in the evening.

Kowloon Park was an inspiration, if a somewhat confusing one: there were so many levels, so many corners, so many amenities, fountains, animals and birds! To top it all, a huge modern leisure centre was to be found at one end of the park where hundreds of people squashed themselves into an outdoor swimming pool like seals at a mating beach. Why did the Chinese love to crowd so much? How could they live under such conditions?

Morris at last found a quiet bench near the fountain, looking back towards Nathan Road. On the benches either side of him, courting couples sat in restrained devotion, so restrained that it could have been meditation or worship. More than anything else, Morris thought, they looked incredibly bored, as if their lives were being planned out in front of them somewhere in the near distance, at the end of the outdoor swimming pool. What would their lives encompass: long hot summers in their conservative clothes, two hygienic children, package holidays, mortgage repayments, the hardship after the 1997 handover? Morris would not be there to see any of their lives. He had long lost interest in people. The majority of them were simply no good: greedy, unimaginative, repulsive, boring. There were only the boys to read light into or the occasional woman who rose above the cackling acquisitive herd.

A masculine figure sat at the other end of the bench and Morris looked sideways for a moment with vague interest. The man was very portly, Chinese, short and shabby-looking but could not be described as a tramp, more a pensioner finding it hard to make both ends meet. He was wearing a light purple silk shirt, trimmed in an oriental lace design around the shoulders, with a white vest showing at the neck. A small pool of sweat gathered just around his collar bone and trickled gently into the absorbent vest. His beaming round face was the epitome of corpulence with jowls apparently about to burst like a full water-sack. Lower down, it was impossible to know where his trunk met his legs as his stomach and thighs ran into each other in a balloon of flesh covered loosely with light blue cotton baggies. A Jackie Cougan hat and gnarled walking stick completed the picture of down-at-heel eccentricity.

"Is-this-place-free?" he asked in a curious phrase-book staccato.

"Quite free," Morris replied with a ghost of a smile, more out of surprise than pleasure.

"It-is-a-very-hot-ev-e-ning," the man continued.

"Indeed."

"Too-hot-for-we-who-are-not-young-any-longer."

Morris shuffled his body slightly and gazed inexplicably towards the far distance, a habit he had acquired from his afternoons on the benches back home to ward off the winos and the nutters.

"You're not selling anything, I hope."

The man smiled the Chinese smile of embarrassment.

"It's only that I've been besieged since I arrived. Everyone seems to be selling something in Hong Kong."

"No I am not selling anything," the man chuckled, more fluently now that he had established contact. "I have nothing to sell."

Morris felt suddenly ashamed of his brashness.

"How long have you lived in Hong Kong?" Morris asked civilly.

"Since the revolution. Nineteen-forty-nine. Is a very long time."

"It certainly is."

"What you do Hong Kong? Holiday?"

"No. Business."

"Business? You no look like businessman. You look like you in trouble."

Morris eyed the man with surprise. The sudden challenge was not malicious. He could see that from the man's constantly genial face.

"What's your name?"

"Me? I Mister Lo. Nice to meet you."

He proffered a leathery hand, chubby, like a child's.

"You live in this area?"

"No. I live Mong Kok. Alone. Nobody left. Wife died. Daughter go to Canada."

"I see. You must get lonely."

"Lone-ly."

Mr. Lo paused and inhaled the word like an exotic perfume.

"Yes. I some time lonely."

"What do you do all day, if you don't mind me asking?"

"Do? I try to stay alive. This is not always easy. To stay alive when you are no longer at work, you need amusement. Amusement is not cheap in Hong Kong.

Nothing is cheap any more in Hong Kong."

Mr. Lo lit a Chinese cigarette without offering Morris the packet. Morris thought this a little unfriendly.

"I read yesterday's newspapers in the morning in one of the so-called parks in Yau Ma Tei. There are many old men doing exercises. To me, that is about as useless as anything. I have never exercised. I have always thought to liberate the body from all that. I am still alive. I find the newspapers in many places. Nowadays, so many people are impatient and wasteful that I find today's newspaper discarded before eight o'clock. I take tea at a snack shop and watch the world go by. There are many people to meet there. I have many friends. Lately, many are dying. There is always a free stool. There are many ghosts."

"Ghosts?"

"You do not believe in ghosts? The streets are filled with them. Many more than the living people. I try not to look but they are always there."

Mr. Lo saw Morris' look.

"But do not worry. I am not mad. Many of my friends are mad at the snack shop. They take tablets. They talk and no one understands."

"So the owner lets you sit there all day, does he?"

"There is nowhere else to go. We disappear at lunch time. Many cannot afford his prices. I, for example."

Suddenly, Morris had what he instantly thought his best idea for weeks.

"Would you like to join me for dinner?"

"Dinn-ah? You invite me for dinn-ah? Where we go? You like the Chinese food?"

"Sometimes."

"O.K. I no like. I like Western food. Like Shanghai. I worked all over the big hotels in Shanghai. Under-manager. Before the Communists came. French *cuisine*. Very good!"

The old man raised a thumb towards Morris, his face beaming with pleasure.

"Look. I have idea. We go Pac-if-ic. Buffet. Everything you can eat."

Morris calculated whether his budget would run to two. In the end, he decided, it didn't matter. Mr. Daswani would simply have to do without his bonus.

"Let's go."

For the first time since childhood, Morris had struck up an acquaintance just for the sake of it—a curious acquaintance on one's last evening: not a boy, or a potential employer or someone to bum drinks from; merely someone with whom to pass away the time and to take one's mind off the dreadful present.

Mr. Lo raced down the hill towards Tsim Sha Tsui. If he paced himself properly, Morris could arrive at a compromise between the sweaty exertion of walking and the cooling effect of moving through the air. There he was, suffering to the last. Hong Kong made White men suffer.

He was dressed, he thought, adequately for any hotel lobby in his lightest but slightly shabby suit and an open-necked shirt. In Hong Kong, no one seemed very shocked by anything—singlets, shorts, sandals. Everything was permissible. Surely they would not demand a tie. They didn't. The waiter of the *Café de Marseille*, dressed himself in black tie, led the men to a well-appointed table and showed him a tantalizing list of victuals.

It all looked so appetizing, even in the dim underground cavern where the restaurant had been appointed. The food was distributed in huge urns along the silk-upholstered walls, which shimmered occasionally as Morris, despite his depression, walked along the tubs in an ecstasy of preprandial gloating. There was gazpacho, salmon pâté and toast, grilled fish, garoupa meunière, filet Wellington, asparagus and Parma ham, chili prawns, roast beef, a rack of lamb, Waldorf salad, salade nicoise, a sushi bar, teppanyaki, tempura, black forest gateau, mousse au chocolat, sorbet and petits fours. Morris was careful to keep some delineation in the several plates he consumed and did not, like many of his fellow guests, mix the pâté, the roast beef, two salads, the sushi and the mousse au chocolat on one plate.

Mr. Lo, however, had no such reserve, amassing a disgusting mixture of food on his plate as if it were his last. After he had devoured a considerable portion of pâté, egg salad, fruit cake, roast duck and rice noodles, he looked up towards Morris, who was picking his way through his modest plateful like a man thrice sated.

"You look like a man in trouble. Excuse me. I do not want to be impolite. I do not know why you should be in trouble. You are a White man and in good health, as I see. What is your trouble? Sorry I say to ask."

Morris chewed his present mouthful thoughtfully before replying.

"I think you could say that I've had enough of life."

"I know the feeling. I have often had this feeling. I have had many hard times. Only habit kept me from dying. You know, habit is sometimes a good, sometimes a bad thing. In Shanghai, when they were selling human flesh in the market and rats were a delicacy, I decided to keep going because it was habit. A bad habit, actually. It would have been better to die sometimes. Now you do not have this trouble. You have a dish of fine food before you and you earn enough not to think twice about inviting an old fool like me to have dinner with you. You must be quite a rich man indeed."

Mr. Lo snorted slightly on a scoop of sorbet which had gone the wrong way before continuing:

"If you are rich, Hong Kong is wonderful. There is no need to be in trouble."

"I'm not rich. I don't think I ever will be. If I were rich, I wouldn't be staying in Chung King . . ."

"Ah, that is typical of your modesty. Do you know how much money I have per month to live on? It is hardly enough to buy the food we are consuming. I live on scraps. My amusements are the stars. I have nothing. You, on the other hand . . . but it is typical also of the White man nowadays. They are always complaining. Excuse me. I do not want to be rude. Excuse. But the White man is at his end. The future is with the Japanese and those in

Asia. The White man is very lazy. Look at the English for example. I have lived there for some time but I got very tired listening to their moaning and watching their decline. Their secret is that they only admire the loser. They have no interest in the winner, like the Americans. But the Americans! They have lost. Years ago. But they still think they are the winners. It is so . . . silly of them!

"But the Japanese are so inhuman."

"Is winning inhuman? Was Victorian England so much better? Were Henry Ford's factories better? Was the poverty of the Great Depression less inhuman? There is nothing more inhuman than poverty. I must have more food."

Mr. Lo filled a fresh plate with roast pigeon, pickled cabbage, egg rolls, cauliflower cheese, potato salad, pork cutlets, lamb kebabs, rollmop herrings and a large slice of Gorgonzola.

"The whole world wants a Walkman, a video recorder, a gold watch, a refrigerator and an air conditioner. What do you want? Happiness. Happiness is wanting the air conditioner not having it. You must make life harder for yourself in order to make it easier. I hope I am not too . . . rude. I feel for you. I am sorry for you. You are unhappy. You are hungry at a feast and I do not know why. I am always guessing. What throws the shadows in your soul? I will help you, if I can."

Morris told him everything—his redundancy, his drinking, his unhappiness in love, his sexual ambivalence. Mr. Lo listened intently, smiling occasionally like a gleeful child.

"It is as I guessed. The Western Man. Too much of everything. Too much hope, too much expectation, too much material. You are brainwashed by your ideas. It is a baggage dragging you to an early grave."

The food came and went from Mr. Lo's plate, six or seven platefuls were devoured with the same intensity down to the last laden fork or spoonload. At last he sat back, loosened his belt a notch and belched.

"You need a woman. Fortunately, in Chung King, where you live, that is not a problem. Day or night, woman may satisfy your most intimate desires."

Mr. Lo's eyes flashed and sparkled below his glowing cheeks.

"Come," he went on, "lead me to the Gates of Heaven!"

Morris had budgeted two thousand dollars for pleasure after the meal. Mr. Lo was more than satisfied.

"With so much money, we could have a night club hostess. But I am not dressed for such sophistication. We must be more modest in our desires."

Mr. Lo led Morris into Chung King arcade, past the Panasonic showroom and the bargain electronics shops, through past the unshaven restaurant touts and the cheap tailors, up the stairs to an innocuous stall selling the sort of clothing older street-sleepers might purchase when they had a small windfall. The owner, an elderly Chinese gentleman with a squint, dressed in sandals, shorts and a singlet, was slurping a bowl of noodles when Mr. Lo approached. He looked up, wiped his mouth on the back of his hand and smiled at the man he recognised as an old friend.

"Ah Chung, we require your esteemed massage services," he announced ceremoniously, indicating Morris with his right hand. "My friend here is very difficult to please."

There was then a lot of merry blackslapping talk in Cantonese that Morris could not decipher. At last, Mr. Lo turned to him to say:

"You are lucky. Not very many Chinese girls will service a foreigner. It is a disgrace for them. But you have connections. You may choose whatever you want. The room is very near and the girl will be there in half an hour. Only one thousand for a short time. I myself will follow your choice. I advise you not to choose too young a girl. They are actually no good. Do not give good service. He says he has a girl of twenty-six, tall, good-looking with an excellent figure and fair skin. I recommend her. What do you say?"

Morris, for whom life had been up to that time less
the fulfillment than the frustration of desire, hesitated to
say yes. After a full minute of deliberation with Mr. Lo,
he relented. Life was suddenly transformed from numb-
ness and tedium into danger and intoxication. Could
things really be as easy as Mr. Lo suggested? He had
often paid for sex before, but never nonchalantly. It had
always been sordid and disturbing. Even now, the spectre
of guilt lurked below the excitement of the evening like a
sinister trip which might be sprung at any moment. As
they stood waiting for the lift with the rucksack people,
the low-life Indians, the layabouts and the ne'er-do-wells
of Chung King, Morris had the sudden sensation of being
freed from conscience, from the guilt ingrained in him
from his earliest years in school, by his mother, his stepfa-
ther, the newspapers, the neighbours and all the sorry
crowd that made up the Australia of the Thirties and
Forties. One had to learn to take life as one found it. He
was an idiotic schoolboy beside the accrued wisdom of

poor, baggy Mr. Lo. His eyes filled with tears, real tears for he had scarcely touched a drop for hours, and Mr. Lo did not fail to see them.

"Do not worry, my friend. It is never too late to learn how to live."

Morris suddenly wondered whether meeting a prostitute in the dank catacombs of Chung King could be exemplary Life. Luckily, Mr. Lo went on:

"This is a beginning. You must lose your shame and your ideas. You Westerners have nothing else. The only problem is that more and more Chinese are imitating you. When you have lost your shame and your ideas, you will then have to gain the grace to have a mistress or two and to enjoy food as it should be enjoyed. But, one step at a time. Sodom and Gomorrah were not built in a day!"

The girl, when she arrived, was everything Mr. Lo had promised and Morris felt better than he had done for years. Mr. Lo was not very expeditious and emerged half an hour later than he had promised from the small but luxuriously furnished bedroom in the secluded apartment they had been led to.

"She was quite satisfactory, one might even say very good," he said, beaming at Morris.

"And now, I must say goodnight. I enjoy tonight. It was wonderful. I leave you a card with my address. You can leave a message at the telephone number. I wish you luck and thank you for a wonderful evening."

And with that he was gone, leaving Morris with a handshake and a piece of tatty envelope with neatly written particulars on it.

It was not after midnight and Morris returned to the Belmoral Raj Guest House to find Mr. Daswani and his friends enjoying a late takeaway supper and watching a noisy Indian adventure film.

"Did you have a pleasant evening, Mr. Morris?"

"Yes, indeed."

"And you will require the full English breakfast tomorrow."

"Yes. Thank you."

"And the baked beans?"

"Oh, yes. With toast."

"I shall wake you at nine, if that is in order, sir?"

"Quite in order."

"Good night, sir."

When he had closed the door on the midnight feast and turned on the air conditioner to smuggle some oxygen into his stifling nest in the Chung King maze, Morris fell onto the bed, exhausted. In his mind, he ran through his plans for the next day: contacting the bank, writing to his brother for a loan, calling round the newspapers for a job and, of course, telephoning Mr. Lo.

After all, suicide was only an idea and could wait a week or two.

W. H. Auden

HONG KONG

THE LEADING CHARACTERS are wise and witty;
Substantial men of birth and education
With wide experience of administration,
They know the manners of a modern city.

Only the servants enter unexpected;
Their silence has a fresh dramatic use:

In the summer of 1937, famed English poet W. H. Auden and pal
Christopher Isherwood set out to cover a local uprising in China.
Their experiences were eventually culled in a journal called Journey
to War. *The first stop was Hong Kong, where Auden composed an*
ode to the city.

Here in the East the bankers have erected
A worthy temple to the Comic Muse.

Ten thousand miles from home and What's-her-name,
The bugle on the Late Victorian hill
Puts out the soldier's light; off-stage, a war

Thuds like the slamming of a distant door:
We cannot postulate a General Will;
For what we are, we have ourselves to blame.

Fred Shapiro

LETTER FROM HONG KONG

MORE THAN THREE hundred thousand American dollars' worth of fireworks exploding over Victoria Harbor on February 14th welcomed the Chinese lunar New Year here, and if the display seemed to me less spectacular than Fourth of July observances over the East River—and far less deafening than the usual pandemonium in Beijing, where this year an officially estimated one billion two hun-

Fred Shapiro is a regular contributor to The New Yorker. *From 1990 to 1993 he traveled through Asia, compiling a behemoth, four-part series on Hong Kong and the Chinese takeover in 1997. This excerpt is from part one.*

dred million firecrackers were set off—I have to say that it appeared to gratify the hundreds of thousands of Hong Kongers who watched with me. There is disagreement about whether this is the Year of the Goat, the Sheep or the Ram: the Asian cycle of years named after animals stems from a legendary invitation extended by Buddha to all animals; years were awarded to the twelve who came to see him, but the identity of the creature arriving between the horse and the monkey is ambiguous, since the Chinese character 羊 can stand for any of these. Red, white, green, and yellow streamers, reflected in the windows of the office towers, drew Cantonese murmurs of "Woo-ah" from those lining the shores of downtown Victoria and Kowloon and packed aboard boats in between. And when the final cacophony of three thousand nearly simultaneous shells died away those in the crowd around me cheered before turning toward the subway and heading home. Perhaps they were simply glad to have something we could all celebrate. The event came just three weeks after a noncelebration—the sesquicentennial of Britain's acquisition of the island the Cantonese called Heung Gong ("Fragrant Harbor").

On January 26, 1841, a party of seamen from the survey ship H.M.S. Sulphur came ashore here to drink Queen Victoria's health, and the following day a squadron arrived to raise the Union Jack, enforcing a concession that had been wrested from China's Manchu commissioners by Her Majesty's gunboats. (Not that the British Foreign Secretary, Lord Palmerston, was pleased with the thirty-square-mile prize, whose indigenous population of fewer than five thousand consisted mostly of fishermen and pirates. He correctly described Hong Kong then as "a barren Island with hardly a House upon it"—a view later subscribed to by Mao Zedong, who referred to it as "that wasteland of an island.") Subsequent agreements with China increased Britain's territorial jurisdiction, first to the four-and-a-half-square-mile Kowloon Peninsula, across the harbor, and then to the New Territories—an area that encompasses the hilly region extending north from Kowloon to the Sham Chun River, along with two hundred and thirty-four more islands, one of them, Lantau, bigger than the original. The Territory of Hong Kong now comprises a total landmass of more than four hundred square miles, and has a registered population of approximately five million eight hundred thousand, plus uncounted numbers of illegal immigrants. Since that 1841 toast to the Queen, one obligation that Britain's erstwhile "Gibraltar of the East" has never neglected is colonial ceremony—Jardine Matheson, the original *hong,* or commercial establishment, still fires a noonday gun over the harbor—and yet the sesquicentennial passed with no Territorial observance at all. The government's principal officials discussed the matter, according to Mrs. Irene Yau, the director of Hong Kong's information services. "And, really, we just thought, So what? A hundred and fifty years is not that big of a thing."

It may not be, at that—now that we have passed the halfway point to 1997, a year that seemed comfortably distant in 1984, when it was agreed that Hong Kong would then revert to China. In line with tradition, no Hong Konger took part in negotiating the Sino-British Joint Agreement by which the reversion was mandated. For a century and a half now, while the colony and its residents have been the subject of negotiations between Mandarin and English speakers, the Cantonese speakers of Hong Kong have gone their own way, which is that of the trader, ignoring whenever possible the governments that their British (and, during the Second World War, their Japanese) occupiers imposed on them. Perhaps that's why Hong Kong seems to me to be the most defiantly Chinese of all Asian cities.

Two years ago, there was a brief interruption in this history of political indifference. Hong Kong has endured rioting—most recently in 1967, when the Cultural Revolution looked as if it might be spilling over here— but when it came to organized demonstrations, as the journalist Kevin Rafferty wrote in a 1989 book, *City on the*

Gain (Hong Kong) has established offices in Toronto and Sydney. Any leftover jobs here will doubtless be filled with the help of international recruiters, who are seeking substantial numbers of *gweilo* (foreign) executives and managers eager to come to what is becoming, in the words of Yojana Sharma, a *Daily Telegraph* correspondent, "a mecca for expatriate yuppies fleeing recession in the English-speaking world."

Emigrating corporations, too, may be coming back— if it can be truly said that any ever left. The first to appear to run was Jardine Matheson, which in 1841 was also the first *hong* to build a permanent building (an opium warehouse) here. In 1984, the year the agreement with China was signed, it reincorporated itself in Bermuda, and this year it announced an intention to move its primary stock-market listing to London, but it still holds about seventy per cent of its assets here, including five billion U.S. dollars' worth of office building and retail property in Central District. Another distinguished house to arrange an ostensible resettlement for itself abroad is the issuer of most of the Territory's currency—the Hongkong and Shanghai Banking Corporation. Although this hundred-and-twenty-six-year-old institution now styles itself on billboards, and in my passbook, as "Hongkong Bank"—in government and financial circles it is referred to even more concisely as "The Bank"—it nonetheless created a holding company for itself in London this year. Yet in 1985 The Bank moved into a steel-and-aluminum skyscraper, which it built in Central District at an announced cost of U.S. $640 million. (This figure does not include the finance charges, or the value of the land and furnishings—or for that matter, the cost of installing electronic displays of hourly Hang Seng financial-index figures in the elevators—and the total amount has been estimated at U.S. $1 billion.)

Since 1984, sixty-one companies have moved their legal domiciles out of Hong Kong, but Hong Kong Trade Department officials say that last year alone the

Territory achieved a net gain of ninety business ventures because of the influx of foreign companies. Many of the businesses coming here were recruited either by Hong Kong's Trade Development Council, which maintains thirty offices worldwide, or directly by the city's Trade Department. Recently, I called in at Central Government Offices to ask the Trade and Industry Secretary, John Chan, how he has managed to actually increase business investments in the Territory at a time when even The Bank was arranging an escape route. "In a way, The Bank helped us, by demonstrating the absolute freedom of movement of capital here," he told me. "Of course, The Bank isn't going anywhere—its assets, management, etc., will still be in Hong Kong—but it certainly made the point to investors that they will be able to repatriate their profits any time they like."

What if China changes the rules after 1997?

"Why should it?" Chan asked. "China doesn't need another thousand square kilometers with six million more people living the way its own people do. If it makes Hong Kong just another part of China, what is that going to do for China? Which do you think they want in Beijing—an international center that is a major source of investment and managerial experience or just another city?"

Perhaps that is wishful thinking, but obviously the people who are investing in Hong Kong now are betting their money on the city's continued prosperity under China. People who are knowledgeable about real estate tell me that it takes at least seven years here to break even on a significant investment. Hong Kong has less time than that before 1997, yet this is not a dying city but a building one, difficult to walk around in because of all the construction scaffolds. An Italian-Korean joint venture is building a polystyrene plant at a cost of U.S. $100 million; the Japanese department-store group Yaohan is establishing its headquarters here and spending U.S. $500 million to open department stores and shopping centers; Motorola is building a plant in a high-technology indus-